A Town Divided by Christmas

ORSON SCOTT CARD

A Town Divided by Christmas

BLACK STONE PUBLISHING

30881 1593
R

Printed in the United States of America

First edition: 2018
ISBN 978-1-5385-5685-6
Fiction / Romance / Holiday

1 3 5 7 9 10 8 6 4 2

CIP data for this book is available
from the Library of Congress

Blackstone Publishing
31 Mistletoe Rd.
Ashland, OR 97520

www.BlackstonePublishing.com

I

*W*hen Spunky was invited to a meeting in The Professor's office, she didn't know what to expect. She had taken two classes from him, but she didn't major in genetics or even in a biological field—she was an economics post-doc, shopping for a tenured faculty position somewhere on planet Earth, preferably a place with flush toilets, clean water, and a good internet connection.

It didn't ease her confusion when she arrived at The Professor's office at the same time as Elyon Dewey. She knew him because everyone did. Elyon was that most tragic of personality types: The relentless extrovert with zero social skills. However, he *did* happen to be a brilliant post-doc in genetics, and he had already co-published two journal articles with The Professor.

"Do you have any idea what this meeting is about?" Spunky asked Elyon.

"It can't be important," said Elyon.

Spunky took a moment to process this. "You reach that conclusion because an economist was invited to the meeting?"

"Well," said Elyon, whose attempt to phrase things nicely was indistinguishable from condescension, "it can't be about *science*."

"But it *can* be dismal," said Spunky, knowing that the reference to economics as "the dismal science" would sail right past Oblivious Elyon.

He smiled as if he understood what she had said and got the joke. She might have believed it if there hadn't been a furtiveness in his eyes.

Elyon opened the door and stuck his head in.

"Elyon," said The Professor from inside his office. "Did you forget our conversation about knocking?"

Spunky was more than a little pleased to hear Elyon getting called on the carpet. She didn't hate him, she was simply glad to know that despite The Professor's apparent worship of Elyon's intellect—*two* journal articles?—he knew how annoying Elyon could be.

"How convenient," said The Professor. "You arrived together."

A Town Divided by Christmas

To Spunky, this was a sign that the Professor had something in mind for the two of them, and that meant that either Spunky would do what The Professor "suggested," or she would have to hie herself back to the economics department to deal with all the one-upmanship and status wars. From what she now knew about economists, if you weren't one of the handful of elite practitioners who were respected by the ivory-tower faculty of the University of Chicago, then it didn't matter what you researched, discovered, or thought up—you would never actually exist in the field.

The truth was that Spunky had already cut bait with the Econites because she was tired of fending off the suitors who thought that because she was an economist, she would get all turned on by some grad student who told her all his plans to work in finance and make his first hundred million by the time he was thirty or twenty-eight or whatever number sounded magical to him.

None of them ever bothered to find out whether she cared about money—she was in economics, after all! And it was especially offensive that not one of them ever supposed that perhaps *she*, also an Econ Ph.D., would reach her first hundred million before any of them.

So now she had thrown in with The Professor, who had begun as a physicist of some note, then drifted into genetics when the Human Genome Project was just beginning. Now he was the beacon of interdisciplinarity, which meant he almost *had* to make room for a "genetic economist," as Spunky once called herself, as a joke.

It was the scientific equivalent of declaring herself to be homeless.

And thus, as a homeless Ph.D., she had to come begging at the table of People With Grants, until she somehow tripped and fell into tenure somewhere. Right now The Professor was the likeliest PWG in her life, so here she was sitting beside Elyon in The Professor's office, waiting to hear her doom.

"I admired and appreciated Dr. Spunk's work on genetically isolated populations in the United States —"

"That was just her dissertation," said Elyon dismissively, as if research done for a dissertation could not possibly contain any usable results.

The Professor continued as if Elyon had not spoken. "I have been given a grant for a proposal I created, derived from Dr. Spunk's work. It seems only right to involve Dr. Spunk in that well-funded project. In fact, I am making her the lead post-doc."

Spunky was unsurprised that in the unspeakably unfair world of academic science, she, who had conceived and executed the entire project, was now supposed to be grateful to be *included* in a project designed to exploit her results. She knew the game well enough by now to respond with, "Thank you," and then wonder how many more humiliating hoops she would have to jump through before somebody offered her an actual J.O.B.

"You left us with eleven American communities, between five thousand and twenty thousand in population, where the retention rate has been highest across five generations, and with the highest rate of return."

"That sounds like finance," said Elyon.

"But in this case," said The Professor ... and then he gestured to Spunky to explain.

This was such a delicious moment, to actually get to explain something to the king of condescension himself. "In this case we're referring to natives of the community who leave for education, military, or employment, but then return before the birth of a second child, so their children remain in the community gene pool."

Elyon narrowed his eyes. "Surely you're not going to expect me to spend time on something as trivial as inbreeding. The verdict is in—it's bad and we're against it."

"This isn't an inbreeding study," said The Professor. "It's something much more subtle. It'll require a gee-woz."

The term he pronounced "gee-woz" was an acronym:

"Genome-Wide Association Study," or GWAS. Both of them knew the word well, because it was the ultimate research fishing expedition. The idea was to run hundreds or thousands of complete genomes through a massive computer data search, looking for correlations of genetic markers. Such studies had helped identify some of the many markers for cystic fibrosis, and Spunky knew of dozens of GWAS projects already in progress.

But they were all medical, looking for genetic factors associated with susceptibility to certain diseases.

"So it *is* inbreeding," said Elyon.

"So it is *not* inbreeding," said The Professor cheerfully. "Dr. Spunk, perhaps you can tell our skeptical friend what we *might* find in the genomes of people who live in one of your genetic isolates."

"Near-isolates," Spunky corrected him. "There are no true isolates in North America ..."

The Professor nodded and waved a hand in acquiescence.

Spunky realized that this was a test. She had done the research identifying almost a dozen near-isolates, communities with minimal intake of genomes originating elsewhere, but had she thought deeply about what *might* be discovered?

She had. She proceeded to spend about ten minutes describing things she had thought of. Finally she reached the one that made The Professor lean forward in his chair. "It's possible that there's a 'homebody marker,' one or more genes linked with a tendency to remain in the native community or return to it."

"A xenophobia gene," said Elyon.

"Absolutely not," said Spunky. "This study excluded communities that have a history of persecuting move-ins, and deliberately includes several communities with a high percentage of people who left and returned. It's the returning that makes me think we might find a homebody marker, if it exists."

"They can't hack life in the big city so they run home," said Elyon.

"With that attitude," said Spunky to The Professor, "how can we possibly find anything?"

The Professor held up a hand to calm her. "His attitude won't matter because he won't be meeting anybody," he said. "He'll be the one doing the genome analyses."

"So you expect me to do data entry?" asked Elyon, as if he were being assigned to latrine duty in the dysentery ward.

"That will be part of your duty," said The Professor, "though I recommend that you use the quick and easy chip method that takes very nearly no time at all."

"Well of course I'd use the —"

Again The Professor talked over him. "Elyon will be available to help you take samples in large-number situations, but you'll be trained in taking uncontaminated samples in one-on-one interviews," said The Professor.

Spunky understood. "Because people in these towns are likely to be suspicious of strangers."

"We sent out mailers and emails to selected people in every town you listed in your dissertation," said The Professor. "We're sending you to the town with the highest favorable response rate."

"Which is?" asked Spunky.

"Good Shepherd, North Carolina," said The Professor.

"Sounds insanely religious," said Elyon.

"And which religion does not sound insane to you?" asked The Professor.

"Atheism," said Elyon.

"So in case you're wondering why I'm keeping your contact with our subjects to a minimum," said the Professor, "please keep this conversation in mind. These are people from the Carolina hill country—the Appalachian Mountains, to be precise."

Spunky was relieved that he pronounced "Appalachian" correctly: ap-a-LATCH-un, not the northern affectation ap-a-LAY-chun.

"Please note the pronunciation," said The Professor.

"Pronunciation of what?" asked Elyon.

The Professor looked at Spunky, and she gave him the eyeroll he was clearly expecting.

"I've noticed that people tend to like and trust Dr. Spunk pretty near immediately," said The Professor.

"People like me fine," said Elyon.

"I'm so happy that you've found such people," said The Professor. "But I believe them to be rare as hen's teeth."

"How many weeks will I have to be there?" asked Elyon.

"That depends on how quickly Dr. Spunk establishes rapport with the community. Because our goal is to get *every* genome into the database."

"Ten thousand people?" said Elyon, incredulous. "Where's our support staff?"

"You are each other's support staff," said The Professor.

"What's our real cutoff?" asked Elyon. "What's the number where you say 'Good enough'?"

"One hundred percent," said The Professor.

Elyon was doing all the objecting, but Spunky was just as skeptical.

"Don't underestimate Dr. Spunk's ability to establish good relationships with strangers," said The Professor. "All I ask of you, Dr. Dewey, is that you not muck it up."

Elyon was outraged, of course. But Spunky wasn't inclined to intervene, because she had exactly the same low expectations for Elyon as The Professor. To her knowledge, Elyon had established something between a feud and a cold war between himself and half the grad students in every field in biology, not to mention the umbrage and hostility he routinely created in a shadow of loathing around himself.

Yet this was the longest that Spunky had ever been in the same room with him, and she was beginning to see that while he was insufferably arrogant about his own abilities, he was easily hurt. He didn't know, apparently, that The Professor routinely goaded everybody, in the firm belief—often stated—that people don't do their best work without serious quantities of competitiveness and adrenaline, which were most cheaply produced by anger, resentment, and fear.

"You don't have to do this, of course, either of you," said The Professor, which was his way of making sure they understood that they *did* have to do it. "And from what I've heard about Good Shepherd it will help you both greatly if you arrive there with a lot of Christmas spirit."

Elyon looked at him as if he were insane. "I'm a Jew," said Elyon. "I don't even have Chanukah spirit."

"Then stay out of Spunky's way, because she even decorates her car for Christmas."

That was the end of the meeting, which The Professor signaled by starting to type something into his computer while refusing to answer or even acknowledge any of their questions or, in Elyon's case, objections.

Spunky convened a second, smaller meeting in the corridor, about twenty paces from The Professor's door.

"Let me make sure I understand the division of labor here," said Spunky.

"I do all the science and you do all the selling," said Elyon.

"It's my job to persuade people not only to let us take swabs and spit, but also to fill out long and detailed question-naires on medical matters, which will be easy enough, and also on personal matters, like why they moved out and back in, or why they think so many grownup children stay in Good Shepherd to raise their own families."

"If that's multiple choice, will 'they're all lackwits' be one of the options?" asked Elyon.

"Yes," said Spunky. "But that one will be hidden away in their average high school grade point average."

"They'll lie," said Elyon.

"No, Elyon. *You* would lie because you pride yourself on the near perfection of your grades since kindergarten. But because most actual humans don't care, my guess is that almost none of them will actually remember, which is why

I'll ask them for permission to access their school records."

"This is a Russian doll of endlessly nesting research into the lives of people who were *chosen* for their lack of ambition and achievement."

"That positive attitude of yours is going to carry us right through this," said Spunky.

"Well, you write your questionnaires and I'll find out what equipment I can bring with me to analyze the samples once you get them."

"I will indeed write the questionnaires, which you will read carefully to make sure they're clear and apt for our purpose. And you will physically take all the easy samples—the people who don't need persuasion to be part of the study."

"The scutwork, you mean," said Elyon.

"Yes," said Spunky. "Because this is not one of those high school team projects where one person does all the work but everybody takes the credit."

"I know," said Elyon. "*I'll* be doing all the science, while you'll be going out and making friends like a supercharged elf."

"You do understand the concept of irony, don't you, Elyon? You do know that The Professor was teasing *me* exactly the way he was teasing *you.*"

"He wasn't teasing me," said Elyon, "he was torturing me. And how exactly did you decorate your car for Christmas?"

"Last year I lent my car to Rajam while hers was in the shop, and she let her boyfriend drive it when they were out on a date. He was drunker than they knew, and drove them through the Christmas decorations on the lawn of the house next door to The Professor's. My car ended up festooned with a combination of Santa, Wise Men, Rudolph, and the Baby Jesus, along with strings and balls of little twinkly lights which had their own batteries, so my car looked quite festive when it was towed to the garage. Dozens of people, including The Professor, texted me pictures of the car and then posted those and other pictures on Facebook."

Elyon looked at her with a blank expression, saying nothing for several seconds. Then he said, "Was Rajam all right?"

"She and her boyfriend walked away without injury. Apparently a lawn ornament of the baby Jesus is a very forgiving thing to crash into."

Elyon nodded. "When we move to Good Shepherd, a town that lives like a stinking blister on the ass of North Carolina, we are *not* sharing either an apartment or a car."

"True," said Spunky. "You will have an apartment large enough to hold all your equipment and computers, while I rent a cubbyhole somewhere. And I will have a car so I can range all over the town, while you will be close enough to everything *you* need to do that you can walk."

13

"If you get a car, then I —"

"You get whatever the budget will justify. If you don't like my decisions, by all means get me kicked off this project from hell."

"If I tried that he wouldn't fire you, he'd fire me."

"Elyon," said Spunky, "twice in this conversation have you given me grounds for hope."

"It was unintentional," said Elyon.

"First, when I told you about how Rajam's boyfriend trashed my car, you actually asked me if Rajam was hurt or not."

Elyon looked at her blankly.

"And the other grounds for hope is this: You recognized that if you tried to get me fired, you'd be the one they'd drop. Both of these show that you have some measure of understanding of the behavior of other human beings."

Elyon nodded slowly. "I see. You think those are both good things."

"I think they suggest that you have some amount of empathy."

"I have all the normal feelings," said Elyon.

"You just don't show them," said Spunky.

"Let me ask you something," said Elyon. "Why does everyone call you Spunky?"

"The Professor calls me Dr. Spunk," said Spunky.

"The question stands," said Elyon.

"My last name is Spunk. It's a natural nickname," said Spunky.

"It's not natural to have it completely replace your first name. What *is* your first name? Is it so awful that you hide it from everyone?"

"Yes," said Spunky. "And that question, however rudely it was phrased, shows that you're capable of speculating about other people's motives. These are all very good signs."

"Name?" asked Elyon.

"If I have your solemn oath that you will never divulge it to anyone in Good Shepherd, North Carolina."

"I so swear," said Elyon.

"Or on the internet or any social media, or by text or telephone."

"You seem to think I have some sort of presence on social media, and that I have someone in my life that I could tell your terrible secret to."

"My name is Delilah Spunk," said Spunky.

A couple of beats while Elyon thought this through. "A Bible name," he said.

Spunky nodded.

"The woman who seduced Samson and then betrayed him to her real lover, who was apparently a barber."

15

Spunky nodded again.

"Nobody names their daughter Delilah. Who looks at a baby and thinks, 'This little girl is going to grow up to seduce men and betray them'?"

"My mother and father were just getting religion when I was born. Mother wanted me to have a Bible name, so she picked Delilah out of a list of 'Women of the Bible.' It wasn't till she was deeply involved in a Southern Baptist church that somebody who had actually read the Bible told her the Samson story and asked her why she thought Delilah would be an appropriate figure for her daughter to emulate."

"Thus confirming my belief that all religious people are loons. Including my own very Orthodox family, by the way," said Elyon.

"My mother isn't a loon, she was simply naive."

"No, Dr. Spunk, *knowing* who Delilah was is what marks you as naive."

"You knew," said Spunky.

Elyon simply regarded her without answering.

"Was there irony somewhere in your comment?" asked Spunky.

"An explanation of irony is even more pathetic than explaining a joke," said Elyon.

"Are you somewhere on the autism spectrum?" asked

Spunky. "Flat affect, off-the-charts smartness, but no practical awareness at all of other people's feelings and responses to your words and actions?

"I have often wished I had savant capabilities, but lacking them, I've trained my mind into a fine-tuned engine of discovery and memory," said Elyon. "And I'm always aware of other people's feelings and responses to my words and actions. I just don't care."

"Until we're ready to take up residence in Good Shepherd, let's meet every week at this time, since obviously both of us are free."

"And these meetings will be instead of something convenient, like sending emails to each other?"

"I don't believe you will ever read an email from me, let alone reply," said Spunky.

"Who did you hear that from?" asked Elyon. "An old girlfriend?"

"You've had a girlfriend?" asked Spunky.

"That's the kind of irony that I employ in order to entertain myself," said Elyon. Then he walked away.

Spunky's first thought was that maybe if she just did nothing, the whole project would go away. The Professor would find some other team for this grant, and Spunky could move back home to Tempe and sun herself on her parents' front gravel while she thought of something she could do with her ambiguous doctorate that would allow her to support herself someday.

But Spunky immediately realized that she could never do that. She would dig in, write the questionnaires, gather the material they'd need, supervise Elyon's equipment acquisitions, and handle the logistics of getting them both moved in to appropriate apartments in Good Shepherd.

With any luck, this could all be done before the first of October, so that the actual data acquisition could be sorted before Christmas.

If everybody was cooperative, it might even be *finished* before Christmas.

Then she remembered her father's first law of adulthood: Everything takes longer.

2

*G*ood Shepherd was not what Spunky expected, but when she tried to think of what she *had* expected, she couldn't figure it out. Had she expected Disney World's Main Street? Or a depressed downtown of pawnshops, nail salons, thrift stores, and homeless shelters where department stores used to be?

Since there was no WalMart anywhere near Good Shepherd, the downtown was still alive, with two grocery stores and a couple of one-off department stores. A florist, a book shop, several salons and boutiques, a hobby store, and a discount store in a building that still bore the name of J.J. Newberry, a now-defunct five-and-dime, in faded signs painted on brick walls.

It was a downtown where people of every income level could come and shop, with not a recognizable mall-store anywhere. Even the eating establishments were local—a couple of diners, a soup-and-salad lunchery, and one sit-down restaurant with a clear intent to seem classy. No arches, crowns, or saucy red-headed girls.

Every store seemed to have apartments above it. People lived downtown.

"So we're not doing genetics here," said Elyon. "We're doing paleontology."

For once Spunky agreed with him. "The town that zoning laws forgot," she said.

"It's like the churches are the tent pegs keeping the whole town from blowing away," said Elyon.

Only then did Spunky notice the churches. She realized that to Elyon, it was bound to look like a large number, but Spunky grew up in a church-going town and so the churches were, to her, like lawns—you only noticed them if they weren't well tended.

There were the normal denominations for a southern town, and none of them looked particularly large. The only church buildings with any attempt to look imposing faced each other across the small town square, and neither one managed to look like anything special compared to the two banks, the courthouse, and the city hall.

But the churches still won out because they both had

steeples, one with a big clock and the other with a big bell.

"I wonder if the bellringer sets his watch by the other church's clock, or if the clockwinder set the clock by the bellringer's idea of noon."

"They just look at their cellphones," said Elyon.

"I'm afraid our mobiles have been bricked in this place."

Elyon pulled out his iPhone and swore. "No bars at all."

"The bars are at the far ends of Main Street," said Spunky.

"You know what I meant," said Elyon. "No reception."

"It'll be interesting to see whether we can get any kind of high-speed internet," said Spunky.

"It'll be even more interesting if we can discover that none of these people have human genes so we can get back to civilization."

"This *is* civilization," said Spunky. "Look at the sidewalks at four on an autumn afternoon."

"Wow. Real pedestrians."

"Exactly," said Spunky. "These people have actual working feet. They aren't just squishy driver worms inside cars."

By now Elyon had located the address of their rental agent, half a block off of Main Street. And it only took a moment for the agent to point out the building where both of their apartments—and their office—were located. Directly across the same side street.

"How convenient," said Spunky.

"Because we'll be dropping in on our rental agent every morning to tell her how we're doing," said Elyon.

"Because we're half a block from Main Street. And a diner that serves breakfast."

"Aren't you the cheerful one, Pollyanna," said Elyon.

Spunky really couldn't let that one pass. "Have you ever actually read *Pollyanna*?"

Elyon looked at her blankly. "There's a book?"

"What, you only saw the Hayley Mills movie?" asked Spunky.

"Movie? It's just—a word my parents used for anybody who was insanely cheerful no matter what happened."

"That's a fair definition," said Spunky. "Don't ever see the movie."

"It's that awful?"

"No, but it makes people with human hearts cry, and that might cause other people to realize you don't have one."

"I cry at sappy movies," said Elyon. "That's why I don't go to them."

It took them forty minutes to unload the van that would be their only source of transportation for the duration of the study. Elyon got the big apartment so he could sleep in the smaller bedroom, run all his analytics out of the big bedroom, and use the furnished living room as a reception area for people coming in to fill out their questionnaires and have their samples taken.

Elyon was working on connecting all the electronics that were supposed to be connected when Spunky announced she was going out for a walk.

"Why?" asked Elyon.

"To see the town."

"We saw the whole thing driving in."

"We're going to live here for a few months, why not get to know the place?"

"And what will you do the second day?"

She ignored him then, and walked to the central square. There was a bandstand there, and a set of weathered bleachers. Apparently this was where public events and ceremonies took place. The bandstand made her think of middle school, trying to get tuneful sounds out of her flute until she liberated herself by not registering for the orchestra or band when she entered high school.

Did Mom and Dad still have that flute? It's not as if Spunky ever looked for it when she went home.

The two big churches that faced each other across the square were both Episcopalian, which in the small-town South meant they were the churches that the well-off people attended. But why two?

Then she got close enough to the second one to see that it was the First Episcopal Church of the Nativity. Wait ... didn't the *first* one have that name?

She walked back and peered again at the sign. First Episcopal Nativity Church, it said. Were they both branches of the same franchise?

Somebody near her chuckled. "Strangers always get a kick out of that."

Spunky turned to face a bald man in a suit. "Oh, is it funny?"

"Not to us," said the man. "I'm Eggie Loft, and so many people hate me that I'm serving my eighth term as alderman, which means I get their phone calls when there's a feral cat or a particularly clever garbage-can-tipping raccoon or a new pothole in a paved road."

"Isn't there a whole board of aldermen to take those calls? And a mayor and a town office?"

"This is Good Shepherd, North Carolina," he said. "We keep offering the position of mayor but nobody runs for it. And if somebody ever ran for one of the other alderman seats, they know that I'd retire, so they don't do it."

"I see what you mean. They must keep you hopping."

"I take care of every problem they bring me, within a year."

"A year?"

"These are patient people. A year is usually quick enough. But those churches—they are *not* a joke. When the Episcopalians split in two, it's like it turned Main Street into a deep canyon. Nobody has crossed over from one church to the other in ... how many years now? Old Dan and Bubby McCoogle are eighty-seven this year, so yes ma'am, the Episcopalians are divided in half for nearly a century."

"But the churches have the same name," said Spunky.

"Neither one would give up the Nativity name," said Eggie. "That would be like conceding the other side was right."

"Right about what?"

"Exactly my point," said Eggie. "I bet you're *Dr.* Spunk, here to find out just how inbred our town is."

"That is not at all our purpose, Eggie," said Spunky cheerfully, "and I hope you'll call me Spunky."

"'I hate Spunk,'" said Eggie, with so much scorn and fervor that Spunky was taken aback. She couldn't answer.

"I suppose you get that all the time," said Eggie.

"I've never run into anti-Spunk prejudice until this moment," said Spunky.

"First episode of the *Mary Tyler Moore Show*," he said. "Lou Grant tells Mary that she's got a lot of spunk, and she starts to thank him, and he says, 'I hate spunk.'" Then he laughed. At a fifty-year-old tv show.

"I've never seen it," said Spunky.

"Obviously, or you'd be laughing too. It's one of the great moments in television history. Right up there with, 'As God is my witness, I thought turkeys could fly.'"

Spunky had to shake her head.

"I guess you weren't watching television in 1978," said Eggie.

"If you believe in reincarnation, maybe I was," said Spunky. "And you aren't old enough, either."

"You caught me. Born in 1983. But my father loved telling that one. *WKRP in Cincinnati* was his favorite show. He never watched *Cheers* because he didn't hold with drinking. Had no problem with cleavage, though—when Loni Anderson was on the screen, you couldn't look at anything else."

"So you were *born* a decade before me, but you grew up in an *earlier* decade."

"That's it," said Eggie, chuckling. "And he always quoted Lou Grant's 'spunk' line because he knew I'd meet *you* someday."

It was her turn to chuckle.

Then he cocked his head and asked a question. "How come you don't use your first name? Spunky seems to be a nickname from your *last* name."

"My first name is Delilah," said Spunky, "which is only one tiny step better than Jezebel."

Eggie nodded wisely. "My given name is Egbert," he said. "But of course you assume the spelling is e-g-b-e-r-t."

"It isn't?"

"My father went to college for a little while, so I was named e-c-g-b-e-r-h-t, king of Wessex in the early 800s. He was the first Saxon king to be recognized as the king of all England. Very famous, at least until the Normans arrived."

"I remember hearing all about King Ecgberht in ... no class offered anywhere ever," said Spunky.

"Hence, I go by 'Eggie.'"

"It takes a formidable name to make 'Eggie' preferable," said Spunky.

"I couldn't very well call myself 'Lofty,'" he said. "So my last name was useless."

"Yes sir," said Spunky. "'Eggie' wins."

"They told me you were walking around looking lost," said Eggie, "so I came out to explain the churches to you."

"Did you think that was an explanation?" asked Spunky.

"I'm quite sure it was an explanation. Remember that it happened about fifty years before I was born. I have already told you exactly everything that I know. There was one church, and then there was two, and they've been fighting like ... like Christians ever since."

"Fighting?"

"No guns, no knives, no ambushes," said Eggie. "That's Kentucky or Bosnia or West Virginia. Here, we just choose up sides and never, never, never regard the other side as fully Christian, or their pageant as the *real* Nativity play."

The fact that he was shaking his head made it clear he thought it was at least a little bit crazy.

"Can't people just go to both?" asked Spunky.

"*You* can, because you're an outsider," said Eggie. "Only you can't, because they begin and end at the exact same moment on opposite sides of the square. And each one faces toward their own church, so their backs are to each other. I can't believe you didn't know about the 'dueling pageants of Good Shepherd.'"

"Never heard of it."

"Then why in heck did you decide to come here? That's the only thing that's even close to famous about this town."

"You mean besides having only one alderman and no mayor?"

"Why pay for more government and waste time on more meetings than you need?" he asked.

"Very sensible. Why pay to put on one more pageant than you —"

28

"Oh, Dr. Spunk, we need those pageants. Else half the Episcopalians would leave town in a huff, and the other half would regard it as beneficial ethnic cleansing."

With a grin and a jaunty wave, Eggie Loft, Alderman, turned away and walked back to the city hall.

Spunky's immediate response was a desire to hurry back and tell Elyon about this weird holy war. Then she remembered that he was, after all, *Elyon,* so she headed for the nearest of the diners and began her exploration of the short-order menu.

3

Spunky didn't really think of herself as good at meeting people, because approaching strangers made her crazy with worry. But once she was actually speaking to the person, the adrenaline kicked in and her brain was able to come up with a stream of very useful ad-libbed questions while noticing every fact about the person that she could ascertain.

Because she excitedly asked rather charming questions, and then listened intently to the answers, people considered her a superb conversationalist. She used to protest, "But I don't actually contribute anything to the conversation."

Most people, being unobservant, replied, "Of course you do." The Professor, however, merely smirked and said, "What do you think people want good conversations to be? They don't want your contribution, they want your raptly listening face, your responsive face, your inquiring face—and the only sound they want from you is a stream of polite burbles to indicate that you're still listening."

Spunky knew quite well that it was *this* talent of hers (which she still didn't really believe she had) that had prompted the Professor to partner her with a socially unskilled science-and-numbers guy. Elyon would do his job, and leave Spunky to win people over to the project.

But *ten thousand* people? That was just insane. Elyon calculated the numbers. "If you work eight-hour days, and we allow fifteen minutes for each interview, which is absurdly low, and fifteen minutes of travel time between interviews, and then we allow an hour a day to set up the interviews, it will take more than eighteen thousand days, and even with no days off, that's almost fifty-two years."

"You could help," said Spunky.

Elyon rolled his eyes—proving that he really had been a teenager once—and said, "Only if we want to be ridden out of town on a rail."

"Oh, come on, you wouldn't be *that* bad at it," she said.

"The manager of that breakfast place asked me to stop coming in because the waitresses were complaining."

"Don't you tip?"

"Bigger and bigger tips every day."

"I can't imagine you making passes at them," said Spunky.

"I'm not sure if I should be proud or offended that you can't even *imagine* me making a pass, but no, I don't."

"So how did you offend them?"

Elyon shook his head. "If I knew, I would have stopped."

But Spunky already knew. It was the punctilious way that Elyon gave detailed orders and then quizzed waiters—and everybody else—to see if they really understood his instructions. When she called him on it once—"Why do you *test* them like this was an introductory course in serving food to Elyon?"—his reply was, "Because that's what it is." When pressed, he explained that he doesn't like disappointment.

When she emailed The Professor with a complaint about the sheer numbers of interviews, he fired back a snippy answer: "Didn't you take statistics? Hand out the questionnaires. Follow up with interviews of a randomly selected subset of questionnaire responders *and* non-responders. With a little thought, we can cut at least ten percent out of that fifty-year estimate."

He was being funny—she had to cut 98 percent out of it because the grant wasn't infinite. But when she discussed his email with Elyon, it took the lad only two hours to write a program to randomize all the selections for them while still making them statistically representative.

"We'll have the complete genome from all of them," Elyon said, "and that's what *really* matters."

Spunky might have retorted that she was so happy to find out that her work was completely trivial while his was "what *really* matters." Instead, she realized that if Elyon believed his work was far more important than hers, he'd stay out of her way. There would be no profit in correcting him.

At first her activities consisted of visiting all the open businesses in town to persuade them to put up posters and stacks of flyers, announcing the Good Shepherd Genome Project:

"It's free, it's quick, there are no needles. It will help if you fill out a questionnaire. Your information will be identified by a randomly assigned number and no one will ever know whose genome is whose. Insurance companies will not be notified of any health information found. Children and babies are as important to the study as adults of every age. If you can't come to the GSGP clinic, email me and I'll come visit. Signed, Dr. Spunk."

She had a nice way with design, so it was all arranged on the page in a completely readable form, and her manner of writing it was folksy and warm.

But she quickly learned that the most important thing she did was converse with store employees until they liked her. Then, when she was gone, they'd *talk* about what a lovely person Dr. Spunk was, and how easy she was to talk to, and how trustworthy she seemed. If she said no needles, there wouldn't be needles. If she said their names would be held back and the results wouldn't be shared with anybody, then it would be true.

She had to replenish the stacks of fliers several times, and by mid-November they had almost five thousand samples. Of course, Elyon could only process them at a finite rate, but it was pretty quick and he was up to three thousand genome records analyzed.

Spunky had conducted about a hundred interviews. If you were generous about the definition of "interview."

But there were almost as many questionnaires turned in as DNA samples, though many of them stuck to the health-related questions only. Biographical information usually started strong and then petered out when she got to the none-of-your-damn-business questions like, Have you ever moved away from Good Shepherd for more than a month? Why did you return?

Maybe a lot of people felt as Elyon had assumed—that when they moved back to Good Shepherd it was a sign of personal failure in the outside world. But the non-responders on the biographical questions outnumbered the responders by a wide margin. They couldn't *all* have failed.

There was one thing about southerners that could be *so* maddening to Spunky. The way a southerner says yes is "Why, that's such a wonderful idea! I'll absolutely fill out the whole questionnaire." The way a southerner says no is "Why, that's such a wonderful idea! I'll absolutely fill out the whole questionnaire." The only way you can tell the difference is to wait and see what they actually do.

Elyon was perfectly happy because he was racking up good numbers in his portion of the project, while she was falling short in hers. It didn't dawn on him that the fact that the people in this hamlet showed up at the clinic in such high numbers was completely owing to her wooing of shopkeepers and clerks.

Nor did he notice that his job was completely mechanical and quick, while hers required insight and responsiveness and observation and empathy and warmth and humor and verbal ability at a level that he couldn't recognize, let alone carry out.

Unfortunately, she was as blind to her contribution to Elyon's success as he was. She thought her interviews all went well, and when she was there in person in their parlors—she couldn't think of them as "living rooms" when so many of them looked like they were straight out of the set of *Gone with the Wind*—they would tell her stuff she would never have dared to ask on the questionnaire.

In fact, she rarely had to ask *anything* that might be construed as prying, because when she simply listened raptly as they talked, they would ramble into stories that were so personal and even confessional that she could hardly believe they would tell them to a complete stranger.

But by then she wasn't a complete stranger. She was a deeply interested friend.

There were no fifteen-minute interviews. It took that long just to get past the iced tea and the homemade rolls and the pralines, which apparently made the trip up from New Orleans to this mountain village on a regular basis.

"If you'd just discipline yourself and keep them on topic, you *could* do the interviews in fifteen minutes," Elyon said more than once.

"If I ever did an actual on-topic, fifteen-minute interview, that would be my *last* interview because word would spread."

"Word that when Dr. Spunky comes over, she leaves within fifteen minutes? That would make you *way* more popular."

Spunky didn't bother to argue. Understanding how to get people talking was something Elyon didn't even *want* to learn.

But as Thanksgiving approached, Spunky found that Elyon was getting fewer and fewer visitors to the clinic. It looked as if they might top out somewhere under six thousand samples and two thousand complete questionnaires. Spunky still had a few weeks' worth of interviews lined up—but over the Thanksgiving weekend, though she had several invitations to dinner, nobody would commit to the time it took for an interview. Determined to work, and imagining that Thanksgiving dinner probably meant the whole day, she declined the invitations.

In frustration, Spunky made her way to the town hall to have a chat with the only expert on Good Shepherd that she knew.

Eggie didn't have an office with his name on it. As far as Spunky could see, the town hall was a museum of Good Shepherd history. Walls in every room seemed to have themes. The volunteer firefighters' wall. The constabulary wall. The town doctors' wall. The plumbers' wall. They had pictures of people dating back to the first cameras that came into town, it seemed, and on up to a few that were dated last year.

Then there was the town government wall. Mayors, aldermen, individually and in groups, with a few framed newspaper stories. But there was no photo more recent that ten years before, and no picture of Eggie at all.

"I just don't like how I look in pictures," said Eggie, who had apparently sensed that someone else was breathing the air in the building and came to identify the intruder.

"I don't understand people who don't like their pictures taken," said Spunky. "If you can go out in public wearing your face, then how can it bother you for somebody to take a picture of that face?"

"I don't mind having my picture taken," said Eggie, "but nobody ever feels the need to take it."

"Not even when you're, you know, making a speech? Welcome to the Fourth of July picnic? Whatever?"

"Nobody waits for a *speech* before they start. Every family shows up to the town picnic and starts eating the food they brought as soon as it's laid out and they said grace over it."

"So the actors come to the nativity pageants and just say their lines as soon as they arrive?" asked Spunky.

Eggie laughed. "Oh, no, those have a starting time. But it isn't *me* who sets them off. No starter's pistol! They wait for the four PM bell from The Church Of—though the people from Nativity Church pretend they're looking at their clock tower—and then they just start."

"Simultaneously," said Spunky, shaking her head.

"How else could we get maximum chaos and unChristian competition?"

"Eggie," said Spunky, "I'm running out of interviews and it looks like half the town is sitting out the DNA sampling."

"You mean you *got* half of them to give samples?" Eggie looked impressed.

"More than half," said Spunky. "But I think I'm also running out of talkative people."

"Not possible," said Eggie.

"Let's just say they're as talkative as they are lonely and unbusy," said Spunky. "And I don't stand much chance of interviewing any of the busy ones."

"Like human beings everywhere," said Eggie.

"I thought if you maybe asked people to give us samples —"

"Weren't you paying attention when we met? The people in this town *hate* me."

"I know, they keep electing you alderman, it's really funny but it's obviously not true."

"It *is* true," he said. "If I walk up to their front door the curtains close and nobody hears the doorbell or my knocking or my shouting, and when I walk around the house I can hear them run to the back door to close and lock it, too."

"Pardon my candor, Eggie, but is it perhaps a personal hygiene problem?"

He gave her a wan smile. "Are you trying to tell me something?"

"No, no, just a lame joke."

"They avoid me because they're afraid I'm going to ask them to help solve a problem."

"Are you?"

"Why do you think it takes me a year to solve even the easy problems? The only way to solve a problem is either to raise money for it or get somebody to volunteer to help me work on it. Nobody *has* much money, and when it comes to labor, they hide from me so well that I've become kind of an expert on pothole filling and pruning trees that are blocking the right of way."

"They don't deserve to have a conscientious public servant such as yourself," said Spunky, "if they won't even help you."

"Oh, they eventually do, some of them. But the ones I can count on, well, I can't go to them *too* often or they'll stop being home when I come over. I have to space it out."

"Well, for pete's sake, Eggie, *I* know how to work, and with nobody talking to me most of the time, I have time to help. Let's fill some potholes."

"Ouch," said Eggie. "That takes hot asphalt. I can only do it when our piece of highway tax money comes in. Sometime in March."

"So people have to drive on rough roads all winter?"

"Everybody knows where the potholes are by winter and they drive around them and yell at me whenever they see me. It was sweet of you to offer, though."

"You must have other problems to solve. Tree pruning. I wield a mean lopper, and I've used pole pruners and pruning saws and chain saws, in my time. Never had a branch fall on my head. Or anybody else's."

"Is that a sign of good aim or bad?"

"The only person I know who needs a branch dropped on his head now and then is doing genome analyses in his apartment."

"Dr. Spunk," said Eggie, "I'll take you up on your offer to help. And while we're working together on putting the fence back up around the cemetery by the highway—a favorite target of drunk drivers, I'm afraid—I'll let you interview *me,* just to set an example for the others."

"That actually sounds rather fun."

"How are you with heights?" he asked.

"How tall *is* that cemetery fence?" she asked.

"The next job is putting up the Christmas lights on the town hall and setting up the Christmas display in the square."

Spunky showed her surprise. "Good Shepherd still puts up official town *Christmas* decorations?"

Eggie laughed heartily. "Oh, darlin', this is Carolina

mountain country. If we want a Christian holiday display, we'll have one. And if somebody sues to stop it on constitutional grounds, lightning may well strike their house when they're away and burn it to the ground."

Spunky couldn't hide her suspicion. "Actual lightning, as in an act of God? Or lightning that comes in a can of gasoline?"

"I don't approve of it, Dr. Spunk," said Eggie. "And it's never happened here, because we have a first-rate volunteer fire department *and* we've never had a priggish litigious anti-Christian fool move into Good Shepherd. I think the name of the town puts off unbelievers when they're deciding where to live."

"But you're saying that fires of that sort do happen among the mountain people."

"Empty houses only. Better than drive-by shootings, don't you think?"

"Am I in danger? I'm kind of a true believer in science myself."

"You don't own the building where you're living, and you're planning to leave, and you haven't sued anybody over public displays of Christmas."

"And I never would, because I love Christmas. The more lights the better. Though I have no patience with manufactured nonsense like Rudolph or Frosty. I'll sue if the town puts up *those*."

"You don't scare me, Dr. Spunk. If you're not a resident of the county, then you have no standing to sue. Some lawyer told folks about that rule around the turn of the last century, and ever since then, irritated neighbors here and there have turned some litigious soul into a nonresident. I think it's a pernicious practice and it's certainly illegal, but I don't know if anybody's ever been arrested for it, and no jury would ever convict anybody for a lightning strike burning down a house."

Spunky shook her head. "So there's violence lurking under the surface."

Eggie shrugged. "Unlike those nonviolent drive-by shootings we hear about in big cities."

She shrugged back at him.

"But if there's a mountain country arson gene," said Eggie, "I bet you'll find it."

4

It turned out conversation was impossible when Eggie was at the top of the ladder, attaching strings of lights under the eaves of the two-story town hall, while Spunky held it steady at the bottom. Spending the whole day looking at the seat of Eggie's trousers was only interesting until she ascertained that he still had a young man's waist and backside, no matter how bald he looked.

Why had she thought he was middle-aged when she first met him? If he didn't shave his head, he'd still have quite a lot of hair, even on top. And the only reason he looked heavy was that his suit didn't fit well.

"Did you used to be heavier?" she asked him once, as they shifted the ladder to another place on the wall.

He looked at her oddly.

"The suit you usually wear," she said. "It's too big for you."

"Oh, that," he said. "My dad's old suit. He hardly ever wore it because after Mom died he didn't go to church, and in his will he left the suit to me and demanded to be buried as he lived, in jeans."

"And you did what he asked."

"The suit was about all he owned," said Eggie. "That and the house, which I live in."

"If alderman is an unpaid position and your father didn't leave you his fortune, how do you live?" asked Spunky.

"From the kindness of strangers," said Eggie.

"I *did* see *Streetcar Named Desire*," said Spunky. "True answer now?"

"I went off to Wall Street and made a killing on leveraged buyouts," he said. "Then I came home to take care of Dad as he was fading, and after he was gone I couldn't think of any reason to leave."

"So you made enough during a few years on Wall Street that you —"

"It doesn't take much to live well in Good Shepherd," said Eggie, "especially if you own your house free and clear."

"You don't drive."

"Didn't need to in Manhattan," said Eggie, "and I don't need to here. I can drive a tractor, but I can't parallel park it with the baler attached." He pointed in a direction that clearly didn't matter and added, "I live three doors down that side street. The house is way too big for me but I keep most of it closed up and I only heat the rooms I use."

"You still remember how to drive, though."

"Haven't checked in a long time."

"Don't you ever go anywhere?"

"I'm going *constantly.*"

"On foot."

"Why get in a car to get from one part of Good Shepherd to any other part? If everybody did that, pretty soon we'd have to tear down some perfectly good buildings in order to make a parking lot. And then we'd have to walk just as far to get to the car as we would to walk on home."

Spunky laughed at that, and he grinned. "These lights won't hang themselves," he said. "But that was a pretty painless interview."

Only when he was halfway up the ladder in its new position did she realize that yes, he *had* told her quite a few answers to her key questions, so she could write them up like an interview. But the truth was that it was just a conversation, in which she had done a lot of talking and even teased him a little.

Was he telling the truth, though? She could believe his workday suit belonged to a slightly heavier man, but was his father *really* buried in his jeans? It sounded like a good yarn, the kind that a politician who secretly wants to be reelected would tell to gullible constituents.

Except that if it wasn't true, there'd be at least fifty people in town to contradict the tale. So it kind of had to be true.

Eight terms as alderman, but only about thirty-four years old, if her arithmetic was correct. If aldermen only served a year at a time, that *still* meant he came back to Good Shepherd at the age of about twenty-six. How long was he on Wall Street, if that part was even true? Did he even have time to go to college first? Surely you had to have a college degree to get hired by a Wall Street firm.

And what kind of firm even *does* leveraged buyouts? Was he an investment banker, giving loans to companies looking to do the buying? Or was he working with his own funds to provide the financing? Or was it first one, then the other? How do you even get started in that business unless you get recruited out of college? So was he some kind of business school wizard? Had he gone to a highly recruited school?

Or did he "make a killing" on Wall Street by earning enough money to come home and live in a paid-for house for a few years. How much money would it take to live here? The cost of living for Elyon and Spunky sure wasn't depleting the grant very fast. If she removed the cost of rent and figured out only *her* costs, a single person could live in Good Shepherd for only a few thousand a year. And that included a few splurges now and then, like a train trip to the big city—Asheville? Hickory? Lenoir?

No, the only train that came through town was a Norfolk Southern freight line. What, did he have to hobo it to Charlotte or Asheville? No, it must be the bus that got him out of Good Shepherd, if he ever had the urge to go. Or maybe, if he really made a killing on Wall Street, he'd hire a private plane to take him from the little airstrip just south of town, the one the crop-dusters used.

As one of her elderly interviewees had explained to her, the airstrip didn't have many planes because the local marijuana growers had to trust you not to see their fields and tell on them.

"But doesn't everybody know who grows marijuana?" she asked old Miz Gaywood.

"Well of course we do, but we aren't stupid enough to go out and find their *fields*."

"Why, are they boobytrapped?" asked Spunky.

Miz Gaywood looked outraged. "These are responsible citizens, making a few extra dollars to eke out a living. Setting booby traps that might kill a child just hiking or chasing a butterfly—that would show a severe lack of civic spirit."

Spunky didn't bother pointing out that their weed might end up hurting children anyway, and her mild response encouraged Miz Gaywood to keep talking, telling stories about how her own daddy gave up being a schoolteacher in Atlanta because *his* daddy offered him a lot more money to come and work the still.

She'd have to put down hooch and weed as more reasons why people came home to Good Shepherd.

Spunky even asked Miz Gaywood about the town's nativity pageant situation.

"Situation?" said Miz Gaywood. "Doesn't *every* town have an 87-year feud between the two leading churches?"

"I won't believe you're old enough to know anything about it firsthand," said Spunky, "but what do you *think* caused that rift in the first place?"

"Not my place to speculate on that, Dr. Spunk."

Spunky roller her eyes like a thirteen-year-old. "If you know exactly how old the feud is, you must know what happened that set things off."

"Well, Dr. Spunk, I'm not telling a secret to mention that it was about the two babies born on the seventh of December in the year of our Lord 1930."

"They just didn't get along?" asked Spunky.

"I don't believe they met until years later," said Miz

49

Gaywood. "So it wasn't them as caused it in person. It was the fact that the custom was to use the most recently born baby boy in the congregation to represent the Christ child, provided the baby was in good enough health to withstand the chilly weather."

"Nobody could figure out which one was more recently born?" asked Spunky.

"Everybody knew. But the younger one had breathing problems and he got a very bumpy trip to Mission Hospital in Asheville. Half the congregation believed firmly that this baby would be blessed and healed in plenty of time to take his rightful place in the nativity. The other half thought it was near criminal to imagine putting a child with weak lungs out in the weather, so the very-slightly-older boy should have the part."

"That sounds pretty reasonable to me," said Spunky.

"Then you're one of those apostate heretical Nativity Churchers," said Miz Gaywood with a wry smile.

"And if I say that the younger one deserved a chance to get better, especially if prayer could hasten his healing?" asked Spunky.

"Then I'd say you're one of those heretical apostates in The Church Of," said Miz Gaywood, and now she was grinning.

"In other words, 'A plague on both their houses.'"

"I wish no ill on anyone," said Miz Gaywood. "But isn't eighty-seven years long enough to forget about a ridiculous grudge? Shouldn't *somebody* have made the walk across the square to reunite what used to be a perfectly happy Episcopalian congregation?"

"What about you?" asked Spunky.

"Nobody give's a rat's tail what I think or what I do," said Miz Gaywood. "I could walk back and forth between the churches for two weeks, buck naked, and not a soul would care about my protest."

"You're still an attractive woman, Miz Gaywood," said Spunky. "I think you'd be a major distraction to a lot of Christian men, so they'd have to arrest you."

"Now I'm tempted." They had a good laugh and Spunky went back to town.

That interview with Miz Gaywood was one of her best—and also one of the last before Spunky helped Eggie light the town hall. She completed a lot of his interview in the process, and her next few interview visits with strangers showed her just how small this town really was.

"Saw you helping Eggie with the lights," said every one of them.

"Had nothing better to do," she answered. "And I interviewed him just like I'm interviewing you."

"But you an't putting up lights while *we're* talking," said sharp-tongued Miz Illa Morgood.

"Will if you want me to," said Spunky. "*If* you provide the lights."

And it was Miz Illa who first said what a lot of folks must be thinking. "He sweet on you? You sweet on him?"

It didn't even take her a second to know she was talking about Eggie. "He's just about won my vote in the next election," Spunky answered.

"He doesn't want your vote," said Miz Illa. "He wants you to run against him. Or run unopposed for another seat, so he can quit."

"He's told that to everybody?" asked Spunky. "I thought I was special."

"He didn't have to tell us, we all knew. Laziest boy ever born in this town. Never does a lick of paying work. I don't know how he lives, 'less he gets nice old widow ladies to cook him dinner."

"Do *you* cook him dinner?" asked Spunky.

"Hell no," said Miz Illa. "I'm old, and I'm a widow, but I'm *not* nice, and don't you go telling nobody that I am."

As Spunky was trying to work her way to the end of the conversation, Miz Illa said, "If you an't sweet on him yet, or him on you, you're bound to be by Christmas."

"And why is that?" asked Spunky.

"I get the Hallmark Channel by satellite," said Miz Illa. "I know how it works, specially at Christmas."

"I'm pretty sure those movies are fictional," said Spunky. "I don't think there's some natural law they've tapped into."

"I think that's the only really foolish thing you've said here in my house," said Miz Illa. "I really ought to make you put up lights for me, and buy them yourself, for saying something so foolish. It's plain that both of you is as lonely as an orphaned possum and you're both tolerably good looking and I think you're sturdy enough to bear him a couple of sprats and even if you can't cook, he's got enough money in his stash to hire you some neighbor girl to come in and cook every day but Sunday."

Spunky concluded from this that Miz Illa had already made the same speech to other people, or heard it from them, so the imaginary romance between her and Eggie must be the talk of the whole town.

Well, if it made people want to meet her and talk to her, so much the better. They'd find out it wasn't true when she left town and headed back to the university, and Eggie stayed in Good Shepherd.

It was only when she helped Eggie put together the stage for The Church Of's pageant that the gossip finally got to her.

Spunky found herself thinking, what if Eggie and I switched from helping each other to loving each other? *Could* she stand to live in a town this small, with all this gossip, and two Christian churches that feuded over the baby Jesus for eighty-seven years?

And why was she even *imagining* a life in Good Shepherd? Was she, in fact, developing feelings for Eggie?

Well, yes. But they were feelings of admiration and respect. Those were not inconsistent with love, but they were not feelings of rapture and glory, which is about what it would take to get her to give up her career as a scientist or scholar or whatever she was, in order to live in Good Shepherd and spawn a contender for the baby Jesus part every couple of years.

Plus, if she lived here she'd have to pick a church.

On that day, building the stage for The Church Of, she asked one of the other workers, a young man named Gilbert, what church *he* went to.

"Repentance Baptist," he said.

"Oh," she said. "What side are the Baptists on?"

"Side?" he asked. Then he saw her looking at the two stages being built at exactly the same time, facing opposite directions. "Oh, this is an Episcopal thing. The rest of us just attend whichever pageant we feel like. A boy's got his heart set on a pageant angel, he's going to watch her show. Nobody keeps a tally. The Episcopalians don't care what Baptists do, or Pentecostals. We might as well be Muslims for all they care."

"You ever lived somewhere else besides Good Shepherd?"

He grinned at her. "If I wanted to be interviewed, I would have made an appointment. You must be getting desperate."

"I am, and you're a nice guy, so why not just answer a simple forthright question?"

"Because I spent my whole time in high school bragging like a fool on what I'll do when I made the NFL, and then I didn't get accepted at *any* college with a football program, so here I still am."

"There's other ways out of town than an athletic scholarship," said Spunky.

"Well, I'm overdue for them to come along with a Genius Grant or Publishers Clearing House, but they keep not seeing my house number in the dark."

And Spunky had herself another interview, because once he started talking, there was no getting that Baptist boy to clam up again.

5

*I*t's not as if Eggie hadn't heard the same rumors about the two of them. In fact, being a local boy that everybody loved, he was bound to get teased about it, and Spunky figured that he must be getting pretty tired of having her around.

He made a joke about it, the day they took down the Welcome to Good Shepherd sign from the east end of town, so Mack Wine, who originally painted it, could fix up the picture of the Good Shepherd he had copied from a print by Del Parson that Miz Illa owned. He couldn't go out and repaint it in place, because it was cold in early December and he was old and well along with dying of something that he wouldn't talk about. So they had to bring the sign to him.

As they were unscrewing the sign from the posts, Eggie said, "I've got to get to the big city pretty soon because if I don't kneel down and offer you a big fat diamond ring on Christmas Eve, folks are going to be so mad at me they'll write me in as mayor."

"So you think we're in a Hallmark Christmas movie, too?" asked Spunky.

"Well, you're a smart solitary educated woman going about her business, partnered with a complete geek who doesn't know she's female, and I'm a lonely, good-looking, hairless-but-not-bald bachelor with all kinds of leisure and a mortgage-free house. And we're thrown together constantly because you keep taking 'yes, please' for an answer whenever you volunteer to help on something. We know how such situations *have* to end up for the good order of the universe to be maintained."

"Isn't it enough that we take care of moving this sign?" asked Spunky. "Do we have to take on the good order of the universe, too?"

"Somebody's got to," said Eggie.

"Not me," said Spunky. "I'm not an alderman."

"But you're falling in love with our crazy little town, aren't you?" asked Eggie.

"I am," said Spunky. "If they'll just offer me a job at the

local university ..." Which was the same as saying, No way will this ever be my home.

Eggie sighed. "I guess I'll never get a woman to make a baby for me," he said.

"Well, if you'd stop shaving your head and let the hair grow in, maybe you'd have a chance with one of these buxom nubile country girls."

"The way *they* see it, I'm halfway through my life already. Too old to scamper about with them, but too young for them to count on me dying and leaving them my fortune while they're still young enough to remarry and have somebody else's babies."

"Now *that* doesn't sound like a Hallmark movie," said Spunky.

"Yeah," said Eggie. "More like Jane Austen or Oscar Wilde."

"You *did* go to college," said Spunky.

"I did, but I read Austen from my mother's bookshelves, and I saw *Importance of Being Earnest* at three different universities when I was growing up because it was worth a bus ride to her, since Mama didn't calc'late to raise no idjits."

"Your mother did *not* talk like that."

"She did when she said she didn't calc'late to raise no idjits."

"Save yourself a bus trip, my friend," she said to Eggie. "You are *not* to propose to me in a public place because if anybody is so arrogant as to propose to me in public without knowing the answer in advance, the answer will be 'no' with a glass of whatever liquid is at hand thrown in his face."

"The glass itself, or just the liquid contents thereof?"

"It depends on how sure he seems to be that I'll say yes."

"So my native confidence will work against me." He looked very crestfallen, and for a moment it occurred to Spunky that maybe he was only pretending to be joking, and in fact this conversation might have been designed to see if the idea of such a proposal might be at least a little intriguing to her.

It wasn't. And pitying somebody for their disappointment would be a truly terrible reason to throw over all her plans and dreams in order to live in a town so small it didn't even have a mayor, just so she could bear a kind, hardworking, but unambitious husband a passel of young bumpkins.

Then again, he *had* made a killing on Wall Street before he was twenty-six. Did you still need ambition after that?

She wondered how many zeroes there were in a Wall Street killing.

She thought about Elizabeth Bennett teasing her sister Jane by saying that she really fell in love with Darcy when she got her tour of Pemberley.

It was about time she got a look inside Eggie's paid-for house, wasn't it?

6

But when Eggie took her by the elbow instead of letting her help with setting up the back wall of the Nativity Church stage, it was *not* to give her a tour of his fine domicile. Instead, he explained that it was about time she got her interview with each of the two big babies who had caused all the problems by being born within a few hours of each other on December seventh in 1930. "Eleven years before Pearl Harbor took that date away from them forever," said Eggie.

Old Dan, whose last name nobody used but it was Lacker, had never married and so had no relatives. He lived in a converted carriage house behind the big house he grew up in, which he now rented out to a young family who were related to him in some distant cousinly way.

"I wondered when the hell you was going to come and stick my tonsils till I gag up some DNA," Old Dan said, greeting them at the door.

"I won't come near your tonsils, sir," said Spunky. "I have better aim than that, and besides I doubt you *have* tonsils because when you were young, they were taking out everybody's tonsils."

"What, they've stopped?" asked Old Dan.

"Well, the number of tonsillectomies has dropped from almost a million and a half per year back in the 1950s to a sixth of that number now."

"Now don't tell me you know how many of every kind of operation gets performed every year," said Old Dan.

"I had strep throat and swollen tonsils just over a year ago, and those were the statistics the doctor recited to me as he explained that no, he had no intention of taking out my tonsils."

"Well, I want mine back, so I'm complete on Resurrection Morning."

"The exact number of tonsil transplants performed every year is zero, and that number has *never* changed," said Spunky. "I studied statistics in college, so I know."

"Sending girls to college," Old Dan muttered. "Where will it end."

It was Eggie who answered. "It better end pretty quick, because none of these college girls is dumb enough to marry an old bachelor like me."

"Me too, just the same," said Old Dan. "It's been a dang lonely life. But at least I've never had a serious income, so I always had do-gooders calling on me to bring me charitable suppers. That's the best part about being one of the baby Jesuses—The Church Of can't very well let me starve to death."

"So that was the pageant you were in?" asked Spunky.

"So I'm told," said Old Dan, but then he looked puzzled. "Except McCoogle and I looked so much alike they couldn't even tell our baby pictures apart. For all I know, in the fracas we got switched back and forth so many times that not a soul knows which is which."

"How did you feel about growing up as a Baby Jesus?" asked Eggie.

Spunky shot him a look and he shrugged. Apparently it was a joint interview.

Old Dan didn't care whose question he was answering. "At first I didn't mind all the attention. But when I got to school, that's when it got nasty. There were boys from Nativity Church that couldn't rest till my clothes were covered with mud, and that took some doing on dry days, I'll tell you."

"It turned violent?" asked Spunky.

"Among the children," said Old Dan. "All the grownups were good Christians and pretended to care equally for everybody—even as they tore the town apart with their feuding. That's why I'm not sure whether it was really me in the pageant of The Church Of."

"The Church Of has the bell, right?" asked Spunky.

"The Bell from Hell," said Old Dan. "Rings so loud you can't hear a word spoken inside *either* church, so I don't know as it makes much of a difference which steeple has it. But I hope that's not what you came to ask me about, because I've answered all the questions so many times I thought about writing up a pamphlet of my answers. Only printing up pamphlets takes money, and my handwriting is illegible so the printer can't set the type."

It sounded like he meant that to be funny, and so Spunky laughed.

He either misunderstood or pretended to. "'Illegible' means nobody can read it. Though I never met a soul as called it 'lejjing,' so why not just say 'unreadable'?"

"For an illiterate old coot," said Eggie, "you sure spend a lot of time talking about words."

"They're the only things I've got to entertain myself with. I talk to myself like a crazy person. I answer myself too. I'd think I was crazy if I hadn't seen that alderman fellow doing the same thing."

"You have not," said Eggie.

"We call him Eggie because he shaves his head," Old Dan confided to Spunky.

"And because my name is Ecgberht," said Eggie.

"I've seen your name written down and it's not a name," said Old Dan, "it's an explosion in the alphabet soup factory."

Old Dan was full of information about a lot of people who were dead and therefore couldn't have their DNA sampled. But family history was part of this study, and in Good Shepherd there was a lot of knowledge about ancestors and ancient feuds and which family originally homesteaded this or that plot of ground. Information that could help them chart the passage of and prevalence of various genes.

She had already got so much information that during her downtime, Spunky was charting the town's genealogy. She could never aspire to the completeness of Iceland's genealogical database, but she was working with less than a tenth of Iceland's numbers, so she could at least try to approach completeness.

"*I'm* doing that scientifically," Elyon said, when he saw her charts.

"You're doing nothing of the kind," said Spunky. "You're

doing statistics about long chemicals, and I'm dealing with the lore of the local culture. You: genes. Me: memes."

"Memes," said Elyon, "are a fancy name for epigrams and cat pictures."

"You tell yourself that, Elyon," said Spunky.

"All that lore of the local culture is probably fiction, anyway. I mean, it's already lore that you and that bald coot are a thing, and after we leave here I bet you become the legendary Indian princess who came to Good Shepherd and got old Ecgberht pregnant and then threw yourself down a well because he wouldn't admit you were the mother."

That was the first time Spunky was actually *sure* that Elyon was trying to be funny, and since he actually succeeded at it, she laughed out loud. But then she thought of something. "How are *you* hearing the local gossip?"

Elyon just shook his head. "I'm not without resources," he said. "When the diners stopped serving me, I asked around and hired a girl who comes in and cooks for me. Cleans a little, too."

"Oh," said Spunky. "And here I thought you were tidy."

"I *am* tidy," said Elyon, "though not quite at OCD levels. I didn't say she had to work *hard.* I didn't say she cleaned a *lot.*"

"So she feeds you and then goes home and fixes dinner for her seven children?"

"Jozette doesn't have any children," said Elyon scornfully. "She stays and eats with me and that's when I find out what people in town are talking about."

"So you interview her," said Spunky.

"I know so much more about her than I *want* to know that sometimes I feel like screaming."

"So you yell at her?"

"Never," said Elyon. "She's a good cook, she's always cheerful, she can read the recipes I got my mother to email to me, and I'd never do anything to hurt her feelings or I'd probably starve to death."

Spunky might have made some remark about Elyon entertaining a young woman in his bachelor apartment without a chaperone, but then Spunky remembered that this was *Elyon,* so Jozette was as safe as an escapee being tracked by a bloodhound with a cold.

Spunky tried eating with Elyon and Jozette, a high school graduate with absolutely no understanding of any aspect of Elyon's abilities or work. Her cooking was barely adequate—her idea of seasoning was either a little salt or a lot of salt—and Spunky got the distinct impression that the girl made it a point to bend over a lot facing Elyon, so he could see down her blouse clear to her belly button. There was never anything between blouse and skin to obstruct his view.

Spunky knew for a fact that not one girl in Elyon's entire educational experience had ever tried to provoke any interest from him, so the poor boy was completely unequipped to deal with all that aggressive cleavage.

He's going to be married or at least engaged before this project is over.

Spunky emailed The Professor about this and received a terse reply: "Good for him. Mind your own beeswax."

The Professor was right. After all, the day a monkey ...

After that, Spunky started taking all her meals at one of the restaurants that had banned Elyon. She was glad if Elyon was discovering his desirability to poor ignorant mountain girls who hoped he would take her away from all this. But she didn't have to sit through the first tedious bloom of love.

Then Eggie started showing up at suppertime, and it took maybe ten minutes to get from "May I sit with you?" to him grabbing the check and paying for it.

"It won't save *me* money," Spunky told him. "The grant pays for all my meals."

"How can I impress you?" asked Eggie.

She laid a hand on his. "You know that you already have. But we don't have a future." She didn't have to explain about their mutually exclusive goals.

Eggie smiled at her ruefully. "Here's the future I see for

us. Dinner and conversation at short-order restaurants until your grant runs out."

"Or until Christmas Eve," said Spunky.

"You really did come here just to see our dueling nativities."

"*I* came here to collect stories."

"You've got mine by now," said Eggie.

"As you have mine," said Spunky. "As far as either of us has been willing to share."

"This isn't going to end like a Hallmark movie, is it," said Eggie.

Spunky shook her head. "It isn't going to *have* an ending. One day the Professor tells me and Elyon that we've got enough data and we pile into the van and drive away."

"That *is* an ending."

"Not all ends are 'endings.' Ours will be more like petering out," said Spunky. "But from now on, I'm going to be comparing every other guy who made a killing on Wall Street with you, and none of them will measure up."

"So you'll remain a spinster until ..."

"Spinster! Not I, laddie, unless I feel like it. I'll just settle for somebody who's obscenely rich even if he isn't the kind of guy who comes home to take care of his ailing father and then stays to keep his hometown livable. Because there's only one of *him*."

Eggie got a thoughtful look as he gazed into her eyes, and she realized that instead of bantering, she had been completely candid, and her respect for him might lead him to a false conclusion.

She needn't have worried, because his response was banter. "I see through your whole act now, Dr. Spunk. You go to school for years and get a doctorate so that gathering data as a post-doc will provide you with an excuse to visit small towns, where you can break the hearts of local politicians."

He *was* bantering when he talked about a broken heart, wasn't he? "Good Shepherd isn't small. You've got ten thousand people."

"That isn't even one Bruno Mars concert," said Eggie.

"Eat your food, Eggie," said Spunky. "I've still got work to do tonight."

"All work and no play ..."

"Makes Delilah spunky?"

"I just remembered," said Eggie, "that the food here isn't very good."

"It's as good as whatever Elyon is having for dinner in his apartment, with less cleavage."

"Jozette's mother, Miz Eliza, is a miraculous cook. Jozette just doesn't pay attention."

"I want to meet the other nativity baby from 1930. If he's still alive."

"I already told you that he is," said Eggie.

"That was yesterday. He's eighty-seven. Things can change."

"If Bubby McCoogle is still alive at nine in the morning, we'll visit him. He may not be as lucid as Old Dan, though. They still revere him at Nativity Church. Lucid or not, there'll be somebody with him."

"Do they do that with *every*body who was ever the Christ child in the nativity play?"

"Only the ones who started a war of icy civility," said Eggie.

Bubby McCoogle wasn't alert at all. A middle-aged woman, nicely dressed, sat nearby on the porch of the old folks home, reading something on her Kindle. So Amazon's reach extended even to Good Shepherd, though Spunky imagined the local UPS drivers making deliveries on buckboards. Eggie asked the woman how Bubby was doing today. She just shook her head and went back to her Kindle.

Spunky sat beside him and tried to explain about the cheek swab she needed, but Bubby showed no sign of consciousness except that his eyes were open. Unfocused, but open.

"I don't hear him arguing against taking a cheek swab," said Eggie softly.

"I can't force somebody to ..."

"This isn't a criminal case you're building. It's just easier to get DNA from a cheek swab than from a beer glass."

"The glass clearly contained tomato juice," said Spunky.

"Maybe he was drinking blood." Then Eggie reached over and pulled Bubby's mouth open, holding the cheek wide.

Bubby gave no reaction and made no movement to shy away or bat Eggie's fingers from his mouth.

"That looks like consent to me," said Eggie.

It's not as if this would invalidate his DNA, thought Spunky. She darted a swab into his mouth, then sank it into the solution and sealed it. She labeled it with Bubby's subject number and that was that. If the middle-aged Kindle-reader noticed what they did, she wasn't objecting.

"I feel like a burglar," said Spunky as she and Eggie walked out of the grounds of the old folks home.

"He doesn't want his saliva back," said Eggie. "Or his cheek cells."

"It's not as if we left a hole in his face," said Spunky.

"We both rationalize our ethical violations so well," said Eggie, "that we really need to go into business together. As the pettiest criminals in history."

"The Tissue Thieves," Spunky suggested.

"They'll think the movie is about stealing Kleenex," said Eggie.

"Which gives away the whole plot. You're right."

Parting with Eggie at the clinic, where Elyon was taking samples, Spunky felt a stab of regret. What if this was the only really good guy she'd ever meet? She might never meet a man who would be such a good father to their kids—though how she knew that kindness, hard work, and selfless service would be good attributes for a father or husband to have, Spunky couldn't have said. She just knew that she might always regret her decision to ignore the sparks between them.

But she couldn't talk to Elyon about it. In fact, she didn't know anybody to talk about such things with. They'd think she was crazy, which would damage her reputation, or they'd blame her father's neglectful childrearing for her madness. Falling in love with a bald alderman in a country hamlet. Here, take a long pull on our Sanity Juice—you're decephalizing too rapidly in the hot sun.

What Elyon actually did was simple. He cleaned up in his office and then his eye was drawn to the new phial of cheek scrapings Spunky plunked down on the desk beside his computer mouse.

"Are you asking me to put a rush on this?" Elyon inquired.

"No, forty-five seconds will do," said Spunky.

Elyon sighed elaborately as he began the process of reading Bubby's DNA. "Oh, by the way, Thanksgiving is tomorrow," he said.

"So I've heard," said Spunky.

"I'm inviting you to have Thanksgiving dinner with Jozette and me," said Elyon.

"Three's a crowd," said Spunky, "but thanks."

"At her mother's house," said Elyon. "Cooked by her mother."

"You can't invite me to somebody else's Thanksgiving dinner," said Spunky.

"Miz Eliza did the inviting," said Elyon. "She's assuming that if you ask around, you'll accept. She has kind of a big dinner. A bunch of people have Thanksgiving at her house. Jozette tells me that if you're invited once, the invitation stands for as long as you want to come. I spent a couple of hours last night after dinner helping Jozette set up tables all over the house. It's like thirty people."

"Like" thirty people? Was Elyon beginning to talk like Jozette? Or had he always said things like that, only Spunky wasn't actually listening?

"What time?" asked Spunky.

"I thought so," said Elyon. "I'm going over at noon,

because Jozette and I are doing tablecloths and silverware. Miz Eliza doesn't trust us with the plates."

"Perhaps she knows Jozette well."

"I think she just doesn't know *me* well enough," said Elyon. He laughed, but he also looked a little embarrassed.

"What, you broke something at her house?" asked Spunky.

Elyon looked away from her, as if embarrassed. "She, um, she says that I can't be trusted with plates till Jozette remembers to wear ... a ... you know ... supportive under-wear."

"Jozette's own mother said that?"

"And Jozette said, 'Buy me one that fits,' and Miz Eliza said, 'Stay the same size for a month and I will.'"

This was the way Jozette and her mother talked in front of Elyon? If Jozette's father was in the picture, he was probably loading the shotgun already.

"What time should people who aren't interested in looking down Jozette's blouse arrive?"

"Something about the turkey coming out of the oven about two. Does that sound right?"

"I'll come earlier. Bring something?"

"As Miz Eliza always says, all you need to bring is your best appetite and pants you can let out."

Compared to this aloof scientist, Spunky realized, Eggie was downright sophisticated. He must have picked up his city manners in New York, while he was making his killing. Whereas Elyon had no manners at all, except bad ones, so now he was cloning a set of manners from a family that didn't even meet local standards.

Well, her job wasn't to supervise Elyon's education. If he got out of town unmarried, he'd probably recover soon enough and be back to his regular unspeakable rudeness.

The next morning, Jozette came by quite early and took Elyon away. As a result, Spunky got caught up in her genealogical charts, referring back and forth to photocopied town records, and lost track of time. The knock on her apartment door alerted her to the fact that it was two-fifteen.

It wasn't Elyon, though. It was Eggie.

"Oh, I'm sorry," she said to him. "I'm already late for Thanksgiving dinner at Miz —"

"Miz Eliza's," said Eggie. "I know, because she sent me over to get you. Though you're not actually late. Turkey came out five minutes ago and she sent me to fetch you, because Elyon was vague about whether you really planned to come."

"I've never tasted Miz Eliza's cooking, but I *have* witnessed Elyon's dinner conversation, so I was kind of torn."

"He'll be at the kids' table," said Eggie.

"He's a post-doc," said Spunky.

"The kids' table is a huge honker of a banquet table where Miz Eliza's children all sit, along with whoever they dragged along. Jozette's the youngest, so I expect that her brothers will make Elyon's meal a living hell."

"Or he'll get talking about helicase and hydrogen bonds and leading strands and lagging strands and they'll die."

"All Miz Eliza's sons went to college," said Eggie.

Spunky couldn't hide her surprise.

"Jozette isn't stupid, Dr. Spunk," said Eggie. "Nobody in that family is."

Spunky grinned. "Well, you've got a point. Book-larnin' ain't everything, is it."

"I figure somebody who gets whatever she sets out to get, and then holds onto it, is as smart as she needs to be," said Eggie.

"The hard part is figuring out what you want," said Spunky.

"Well, get crackin' on that, lassie," said Eggie. "Time's a wastin'."

"Oh, there's a deadline?"

"Santa Claus comes to the Christmas parade on the Saturday after Thanksgiving and if you don't know what you want, he shines you on."

"Who plays Santa?" asked Spunky.

Eggie raised his eyebrows. "'Plays' Santa?"

Spunky gave him the chuckle he was asking for, and then said, "You called me 'lassie.'"

"Because you've called me 'laddie' a couple of times so I thought we were pretending to be Scottish."

"No, no," said Spunky, laughing in embarrassment. "Just something in my family."

During this conversation, Eggie had been deftly closing up Spunky's pens and now he was holding out her coat to shrug into. Then he opened her apartment door and closed it behind them.

"Did you lock it?" asked Spunky.

"I'm sorry, didn't you know you were in Good Shepherd, North Carolina?" he said.

"I can't just leave it unlocked —"

"All the expensive equipment is downstairs in Elyon's rooms, but nobody wants to steal your stuff anyway. Where would they sell it?"

Spunky held tightly to his offered arm once they got outside, because last night's snow was of a loose, wet, and slippery variety.

"So you don't want to fall," said Eggie.

"That's my plan."

"And you're clinging to my arm because you are determined to fulfill your plan," said Eggie.

"I am," said Spunky. "And I'm not letting go no matter how much you goad me."

"As long as I get my arm back when it's time to eat, because I'm clumsy with a spoon in my left hand."

"I'll change sides if you want," said Spunky, "but I'm left-handed, and I'm not sure if I can rely on the combined strength of our nondominant arms."

"What if I just promise that if you fall, I'll fall down too."

"It's not as humiliating if you do it on purpose."

"It's not humiliating at all if I do it to impress a girl."

"Or to mock one by imitating her," said Spunky.

"No, *that* would shame me. So hold on tight, lassie, and tell me about this 'family thing' about pretending to be Scottish."

"My mother always wanted to travel the world," said Spunky. "But there was never any money or any time, for that matter, so she read about other cultures. She had a brief Scottish phase, where she greeted us every morning and after school in a thick brogue that sounded perfectly authentic to me at the time. And when Dad finally got her to stop, my brothers and I had already picked up 'laddie' and 'lassie,' and we could all recite 'Wee, sleekit, cow'rin, tim'rous beastie, O what a panic's in thy breastie!'"

"That's a pretty good brogue. A little thick, but Bobby Burns pours it on himself."

"My brothers only recited it to have an excuse to say 'breastie,' which they did *not* pronounce in the Middle English way, '*bray*-stee.'"

"So your mother's wanderlust only took her to Imaginary Glasgow?"

"Oh, no. She collected sayings from other cultures. There was one from East Africa that became a catch phrase in the family. 'The day a monkey.' One of us would say it and everybody else would break up laughing."

"'The day a monkey' *what?*" asked Eggie.

"Oh, it's—well, when something's *going* to happen, no matter what you do to prevent it, then in Swahili you'd say, 'The day a monkey is fated to die, all trees are slippery.'"

Eggie laughed. "Yeah, that's good, that's a good one. Has your mother got any others?"

"She had hundreds, but we didn't adopt them all as family sigils. Oh, here's one. I say this one, too, when I'm not paying attention to the fact that it isn't a saying in English. If somebody's a complete screw-up—not clumsy, but grimly determined to do everything the wrong way so failure is guaranteed—then Mom would say, 'Headin' to the sea.'"

"Help me make sense of that."

"We always shortened her sayings. The whole thing is, 'He goes into the sea to get dry,' or something like that. Farsi, I think, or maybe Turkish. She went through those at kind of the same time, which makes no sense except that they have Islam in common."

"And coasts on two different seas."

Spunky nodded and smiled. "I never thought of that as something Iran and Turkey have in common, but yes, though technically we could say that Turkey borders on *three* seas."

"Black Sea, Mediterranean ..."

"Aegean," said Spunky.

"Show-off. Blathering post-doc. The Aegean is *part* of the Mediterranean, but the Black Sea isn't."

"Iran coasts on the Caspian *Sea* but the Indian *Ocean*,"

"The Persian Gulf," said Eggie.

"A gulf not a sea," said Spunky in mock triumph. "And also a part of the Indian Ocean. Don't ever call me wrong, laddie, because I will rub your nose in it forever."

"I have no doubt of it," said Eggie. "I have no such fragile ego needs. I'm perfectly content to know that you're wrong, yet never mention it again."

Spunky laughed.

They walked in silence for a while, because the route Eggie was choosing involved snow on top of a muddy, rooty path for a while, with low branches that dumped snow down Spunky's neck when she bumped into them.

"Couldn't help but see several charts laid out on your table," Eggie said.

"Are you serious that you don't know what they are?"

"I knew all the names instantly, so of course I knew. You're charting all of our inbreeding."

"I am not," said Spunky. "People always think that but come on. Demographically speaking, the entire world is inbred. Most people can't go back six generations without having the same person pop up in two different places on their pedigree. Everybody on Earth is related to everybody else, and not all that distantly."

"I guess there's nobody for us to mate with but other humans," said Eggie.

"Well, our first ancestors weren't all that fussy. Everybody of European and Asian and Amerindian descent has a decent amount of Neanderthal DNA. It doesn't help us or hurt us, so it's just along for the ride. Then the East Asians and Amerindians also have Denisovan DNA, so—two different groups of humans interbred with us."

"Still humans."

"A source of much argument," said Spunky.

"Among bigots who can't stand to think we aren't a different species from 'cave men.'"

"Nobody says 'cave men' anymore," said Spunky.

"Well, not after that Geico ad," said Eggie. "But they still *think* it. I've heard of Neanderthals but they didn't teach me about that other group back in school."

"Denisovan. From the name of the cave where their DNA was found. In the bones of a child."

"Not just eastern Neanderthals?"

"We've sequenced enough different Neanderthals that we can say with some certainty that the Denisovans were their own branch-off from the parent stock that left Africa."

"I feel pretty ignorant, here," said Eggie.

"Was I supposed to make you feel smart?" asked Spunky, with chip-on-her-shoulder insouciance.

"Hickety-heck no," said Eggie. "It's like with dinosaurs and planets and the names of countries. They keep changing them and I can't keep up."

"I have a degree in economics but I have only the vaguest idea of what you did to make your killing on Wall Street."

"Oh, right. That's complicated. Like a lot of people who make their killing on Wall Street, I made friends with an older guy with a lot of influence. He let me in on a couple of deals so that starting with no capital except a pittance of savings, I found myself as principal stockholder of a couple of firms. And because I knew how to convert those companies into moneymakers, I made that stock rise in value and then sold at a reasonable time and left."

"Your benefactor—was he miffed that you didn't keep going?"

"I went and saw him on my way out of town to take care of Dad," said Eggie. "He said, Good for you, Bert—they called me Bert there—and he said, Wish I'd had the spunk to do the same. Enough is enough, but most people think 'enough' means whatever scraps you leave for the other guy."

"Come on," said Spunky.

"Come on what?" asked Eggie.

"He didn't say 'Wish I'd had the *spunk* to do the same.'"

"Oh. I think he did, but I don't have an eidetic memory, and maybe having this beautiful brilliant slippery spinstery post-doc clinging to my arm made me replace 'guts' or 'balls' with 'spunk.' Cliffs of fall."

Spunky stopped abruptly, which almost made them fall. It took a moment to recover balance. "What?" asked Eggie.

"Did you really say 'Cliffs of fall'?"

Eggie laughed. "Oh, yeah. Your family has its things, and so does mine. My father thought Gerard Manley Hopkins was the greatest poet who ever lived. 'Oh the mind, mind has mountains; cliffs of fall —"

Spunky finished the couplet. "Frightful, sheer, no-man-fathomed. Hold them cheap ..."

And Eggie joined her: "Hold them cheap may who ne'er hung there."

"That's as far as I can go from memory," said Spunky. "Don't know why that stuck in my mind, but I could never memorize an entire Hopkins poem except 'Margaret, are you grieving ...'"

And again he joined in as they recited together, "... over Goldengrove unleaving? Leaves like the things of man, you with your fresh thoughts care for, can you?"

And suddenly Spunky couldn't go on because she was weeping. Not little tear-in-the-eye stuff like at a sad or happy movie, but full on weeping, sobbing into his sleeve as she turned her face into his shoulder.

"Wow," Eggie whispered. "Poetry really gets to you."

"It's about dying," said Spunky, "written by a poet who absolutely believed in resurrection."

"'It is the blight man was born for," said Eggie. "It is Margaret you mourn for."

"But it isn't," said Spunky. "It's my mother, making us memorize a poem every week. She got to choose the poet. My brothers all ignored her choices, though, so they recited

85

perfectly awful stuff from Ginsburg. Or Herrick, 'Whenas in silks my Julia goes.'"

"I bet your mother just laughed," said Eggie.

"How did you guess that?"

"Because come on, they found those poems *on their own* and then memorized them. What's not to love?"

"They found Dickey, too, because his name sounded schoolboy-dirty. 'Warm in such braces, mentioning grasses, grinning disgraces.' For a year after that, Mom called my brothers, individually and as a clump, 'Grinning Disgraces.' Spunky, would you call the Grinning Disgraces in for dinner?"

"OK, that's it. I loved my mother but can't I at least pretend your mother was my favorite aunt?"

"You may have her as your aunt because she had no nephews. Just sons."

"And now you're through crying?" he asked.

"So I'll come in to Thanksgiving dinner with red eyes and wet cheeks and everyone will have to pretend they don't notice —"

"Have you forgotten where you are? They'll accuse me of making you cry and call me Monster all day, and you'll be something like Weepy or Boo-Hoo or Damsel."

"Now's when all my sociological training comes into

play," said Spunky. "I'm going to own this and make it my own. Is that the house?" She pointed to a big ramshackle mountain of weathered wood just down a little more slope and past the end of the trees.

"You guessed it," said Eggie, "since after that house there's a cliff and a rill and then it's deer and bears and raccoons all the way to Tennessee."

"I also see that there's a perfectly serviceable road that looks almost paved or at least macadamed, but you took me through the slippery woods instead."

"And you clung to my arm the whole time, keeping me warm. My folks didn't have no stupid children, missy."

"Missy not lassie now," said Spunky.

"You go by Spunky. I can call you anything I want."

They were there, and Eggie just swung the door open, no knock or anything. Inside everybody was moving toward the tables, as if the sight of them through a window had been the signal for the feast to start.

It was plain enough that the woman with a gravy-covered wooden spoon and a spattered apron and flour in her hair was Miz Eliza, and Spunky was not surprised at all that she greeted her—the first words the woman had ever addressed to Dr. Spunk—by saying, "What did our lazy alderman do to make you cry?"

"Gave me an Indian burn on my arm," said Spunky, filling her voice with outrage. "And a noogy right on the top of my head."

"So he thinks he's your big brother," said Miz Eliza. "Figures, with the dumb ones."

"I don't suppose anyone cares to know what she did to me," said Eggie.

"Not a one of us," said Miz Eliza. "And besides, you're saying the prayer and we're all hungry so do it. And remember that everybody in this room says their own prayers, complete with all kinds of thank-yous to the Lord of Hosts, so if your prayer could end while the turkey's still warm we'd all be grateful."

"And if you'd stop raggin' on me, thou importunate Vieille Dame, I could begin, which will certainly bring me closer to ending the prayer." And right there in the doorway, which was still slightly ajar behind them, and with his arm still around Spunky's shoulders, he launched into a prayer as sweet as any that Spunky had ever heard, ending with the words, 'And let there be no more tears shed in this house today, except of joy in the fellowship of good souls and the memory of beloved ones who can't be with us."

The room was filled with a strong "amen" from everybody—well, most people. Spunky couldn't actually see

Elyon, but it would be hard to imagine him saying amen to any kind of prayer, least of all a Christian one.

Then again, he did know his scriptures, in Hebrew at least, so maybe he bowed to local custom when he was among believers in the Book.

The food was everything Eggie had bragged on and Elyon had promised, and as Spunky watched Eggie during the meal she kept forgetting to eat, because he not only knew everybody seated anywhere nearby, but also liked them and cared about them and asked questions about their lives and their relatives and their pets and their projects and their jobs. And then he listened to what they had to say, and laughed at their jokes, and a couple of times became grave when they spoke of things they had suffered.

He was deft at comforting people. Not the way most people did, by trying to cheer them up, which is usually offensive to somebody who's really down, because "cheering up" is about making everybody else feel better so they can ignore you again.

Instead, to the boy who was clearly sad about losing the girlfriend that Eggie asked about—"Oh, she's off to college, sir, and I don't figure she'll come back much from Boone, if she didn't come for Thanksgiving"—Eggie only gripped his arm a moment longer, saying, "We'll all miss her, but you'll miss her most of all, I think." And then the boy fled to avoid shedding any tears in front of everybody, but as Spunky saw it, Eggie had just validated him, had just said, You're right to love her, and we who love *you* recognize your suffering and respect it. He didn't offer stupid encouragement and he didn't tell him he'd get over it and there was nothing about how many fish are in the sea or how the wounds of the young heal fast or gibes about how a bit of time under the mistletoe would cure what ailed him.

Eggie's genius, come to think of it, was in all the stupid things he chose *not* to say.

And then Spunky thought of their whole bantering, flirting conversation as they walked here, and her sudden rush of tears when they quoted a poem that brought back all her grief over her mother's death, and how kindly and gently he helped her become ready to face a house full of people.

People who were not, after all, strangers, though she hadn't yet interviewed them all.

Nobody here would consider me to be a genuine citizen of this town, she thought, but nor am I a stranger to them. And yes, I worked hard to reach this point, but I also had this amazing man smoothing the way for me. How did anyone ever say no to him when he asked them to help with some community project? How had he lasted this long without being married?

Was it possible that he was right, that young women shunned him because he was balding? Bald shmald, the man at least had a fine set of teeth; surely that moved him to the front of the herd.

Then a thought popped into her mind.

He isn't married because he was waiting for me.

That was when she dove back down into her plate, blushing, and methodically tracked down and consumed every scrap of food remaining.

7

I'm not an anthropologist, Spunky reminded herself. I'm not here to study their culture, and I have no ethical rule of non-interference. If I fall in love with the town's main public servant, and he by some chance also falls for me, it won't change anybody's DNA or behavior patterns or culture or anything.

Except for that tiny lingering part of me that wants to avoid the emotional devastation of leaving here, knowing that I won't come back and that he can't follow me.

I'm just not a one-Christmas-season kind of girl, Spunky realized.

Having never been in love or anything close to it, she hadn't known how it would hit her.

Now she knew.

It was all-consuming. Ever since that snowy flirty walk to

Thanksgiving dinner, ever since she had cried into his shirt and felt his arm around her while he prayed for the whole gathering and watched him work magic in the lives of the people around him, all she could think about was him, except when she absolutely *had* to talk to somebody or do some job, and even then he would creep into her thoughts and distract her.

"Leave me alone," she said to him when she responded to a knock on her apartment door and there he was. "I have work to do."

His reply was to kiss her quite thoroughly and then step past her to stand over the table, looking at the charts. The one on top was the master chart, tracking the families that were most intertwined. She used yellow highlighter to draw the connections when somebody showed up in more than one place—as one family's child, as another family's son- or daughter-in-law.

"Good thing I know you're not tracking our inbreeding."

Still a little cloud-niney from the kiss, Spunky floated over to stand, not beside him—too dangerous to her ability to function mentally!—but across from him. "What I'm tracking," she said, "is Episcopalians."

"The rich people," he said. "Typical historical approach."

"The people divided by the nativity pageant in 1930," she corrected him. "Look at all the intermarriage through the whole Episcopalian community before the church divided. And afterward, not one extra-congregational marriage."

"Lack of exogamy going to be a problem, do you think?"

"Before the war in Bosnia, Serbs and Croats and Muslim Bosnians intermarried like crazy," said Spunky. "Since the war, it took fifteen years before the first interfaith marriage, and it made international headlines."

"Um, nobody's been massacred in a football stadium in Good Shepherd."

"Ignoring the fact that Good Shepherd has no football stadium, just two sets of bleachers at the high school, this is exactly what I'm fascinated by. Nobody's been killed here. It isn't a war. People don't even hate each other, or at least everybody's civil."

"As long as they all stay to their side of the street, so to speak," said Eggie.

"Atrocities, massacres in Bosnia, and fifteen years later, at least one marriage. Bad tempers and building a second church with a clock instead of a bell, plus two pageants at the same time for eighty-seven years, not a drop of blood shed, and *no* intermarriage."

"In a place this small and isolated," said Eggie, "I guess grudges last longer."

"Eggie," said Spunky. "There has to be more to this

than arguments over who gets to play the Baby Jesus."

"We'll never know," said Eggie. "All the people who were making the decisions then are dead."

"That Christmas pageant divided this town. Probably for at least a century. What is it that nobody's telling to the outsider who's here to study the genes of Good Shepherd?"

Eggie stood there in silence, looking down at the chart.

Spunky knew him well enough to expect that he had already figured out how to change the subject completely, and was only hesitating because he knew she'd see through the attempt and be either angry or hurt.

To her surprise, he didn't change the subject at all. "Spunky, you've finally put into words something that I've wondered about my whole life. I mean, even as a kid, when my parents first tried to explain why there were two Episcopalian churches in town and two Nativity pageants, I said to them, 'Well, that's stupid. Why don't they just act like grownups and get back together?'"

"I am not surprised that you were a preternaturally wise child," said Spunky.

"I *am* surprised that you expect a Wall Street guy to know the word 'preternaturally.'"

"I knew that if you didn't know the word, you would guess its meaning from context."

"I knew the word," said Eggie. "I just never heard anybody say it out loud."

"So you agree with me that there has to be more to this," said Spunky.

"I think *somebody* on each team must know what the real grievance was," said Eggie, "but I will never be in the chain of custody for that secret, and neither will you."

"And in the meanwhile, the dueling pageants are Good Shepherd's only claim to fame," said Spunky. "I'm surprised nobody's got some Hong King company to make a bunch of two-pageant snow globes to sell to tourists."

Eggie shook his head. "I've let it be known over the years that if any merchant starts commercializing our town's division, they will suddenly find themselves dealing with all kinds of inspections and infractions and fines and liens. *Nobody's* going to have a vested interest in keeping it going."

"So you're tougher than you look," said Spunky.

"I don't look tough at all," said Eggie. "*You* look tough."

"I think women aren't ever called 'tough.' I think the term for us is feisty. Witchy."

"Spunky," said Eggie, adding to the list.

Spunky frowned. "That moves me from the realm of toughness to the playpen of cuteness."

"Cute as a bug," said Eggie.

"My rule is never to hit anybody," said Spunky. "Please don't goad me into changing that policy."

"Still figuring out what kind of bug you're as cute as," said Eggie. "A mantis? A hornet? A horned dung beetle?"

That took her aback. "Not just a beetle, but a *dung* beetle? Not just a dung beetle, but a *horned* dung beetle?"

"World's strongest insect," said Eggie. "It can lift the equivalent of *me* lifting six full double-decker buses. I'll find you the reference online if you don't believe me. I promise it wasn't in a Buzzfeed slideshow."

"I can't lift more than two buses at a time, empty," said Spunky.

Eggie ignored her. "Technically the bullet ant has a more painful sting than a hornet, but nobody knows what a bullet ant is, and we know hornets well enough that getting a bunch of people mad is 'stirring up a hornet's nest.'"

"You are a font of information today," said Spunky.

Eggie looked rueful. "I'm trying to find at least one thing you didn't already know every day, so that you'll keep conversing with me."

"Well, so far you're batting zero," said Spunky, "because I knew every one of those facts."

"You didn't know that as a child I didn't believe that the town division was really about the babies."

"Eggie, what are we doing?"

"Standing across a table from each other pretending that we haven't fallen in love like a couple of moonstruck teenagers."

"I know that you're not moving away from this town," said Spunky.

"Seems unlikely, in the foreseeable future," said Eggie.

"And after this grant, I don't know what career path I could possibly follow that would ever bring me within a hundred miles of here."

"You could open a Taco Bell franchise," said Eggie. "We don't have a single Mexican food establishment here. When Taco Bell opened in Romania a few years ago, it became the most successful business in the whole country. I made a lot of money from that. Lines around the block. We're like Romania here—starved for ground beef and hot sauce."

"I don't love you enough to get into the food service business just to stay nearby," said Spunky. "There isn't enough love in the history of the world to get a woman as smart as me to do that."

"That's why I only dated stupid women," said Eggie. "Till now."

"In case you haven't noticed, we've never had a date," said Spunky.

"We've had dozens of dinners together, we've worked together on how many projects now? And don't forget walking in the woods on a snowy afternoon."

"Not one of those was a date," said Spunky. "Most of the time I had no idea you were coming."

"But *I* knew I was going to see you, and I spent the day counting the hours and minutes till then, so to *me* it was a date."

Spunky tried not to smile. "You were dating me, but I wasn't dating you?"

"There's no point in looking for precision" said Eggie. "This isn't physics, it's propagation of the species."

"We haven't *done* any propagating," said Spunky.

"All the hormones pumping through us, telling us that we must find a way to live with each other forever, preferably in close physical contact, evolved in order to propagate the species. So even if we fail to propagate, our genes insist on making us try. Right, O Expert on the Human Genome?"

"The more we know about genetics," said Spunky, "the less we understand about love."

"That's so disappointing," said Eggie.

"It's like religion," said Spunky. "Some things we have to learn on our own."

"On my own? Then what was Sunday school about for all those years?"

"It wasn't about love," said Spunky.

"If I climb over the table to kiss you," said Eggie, "I'll make a mess of all these charts you've been working so hard on."

"Then I suggest you stay on the floor and propel yourself *around* the table, using feet."

"Do you have any idea how long that will take?" asked Eggie.

She walked around the table with all the dignity of a doctor about to give a favorable prognosis to a patient. Not hurrying, but unable to conceal her eagerness. "I can't marry you," said Spunky.

"What language are you speaking now?" asked Eggie. "I don't understand a word."

Then she reached him and words were pretty much impossible for a while.

8

Work went on. Interviews happened. More and more people found time during holiday preparations to come down and get swabbed. Elyon managed to look at the screen between meals and see what the computer was finding in its searches through the growing Good Shepherd database. The Professor seemed to be happy with the progress they were making.

Everybody in town seemed to accept that Spunky and Eggie were a couple, and now that it was true, nobody teased them about it. Teasing an unmarried couple about being in love is how a community pushes them to marry. Spunky understood that in general, any culture that didn't encourage procreation was going to be out-propagated by another culture that did. But in particular, between her and Eggie, there was still a lot of territory to cover.

They put a rigid five-minute cap on any activity that Eggie's mother would have called "necking," because, as Eggie explained, "We're marrying folk, in our family. No child should grow up doing the arithmetic on his birth date vis-a-vis his parents' anniversary."

But the restriction wasn't really about protecting children that would probably never be conceived. The restriction was to avoid making any commitment, spoken or implied. Eggie and Spunky were "keeping company," as Miz Eliza put it when Spunky interviewed her.

"What about Jozette and Elyon?" asked Spunky.

"What about them?" asked Miz Eliza.

"Are they keeping company?" asked Spunky.

"Are you his sister or something?" asked Miz Eliza. "Because Jozette thinks of you as her main rival in trying to win the boy's heart."

"As far as I've ever been concerned, Elyon's heart, now that we know it exists, is for any taker. I never would have guessed it, but Elyon seems to really care for your daughter."

"As his non-sister," said Miz Eliza, "what chance does Jozette have to be happy with him?"

"It depends on how adaptable she is," said Spunky.

"Meaning?"

"His brain is going to take him into a top-flight math or econ department in a major university. Academic life is full of constant status wars, and the spouses play right along with the actual professors. Jozette's smart but she's not educated at the level that other faculty wives will be. Can she adapt? Can she hold her own?"

Miz Eliza smiled. "Nobody ever beats Jozette at anything," said Miz eliza. "Because until she wins, the game can't end."

"I'll take that as a yes. But you have to remember—Jozette is the first bosom that has ever danced before Elyon's eyes. I can't promise he'll be faithful in the long run.

"That's Jozette's problem," Miz Eliza said thoughtfully. "For all I know, she might be planning to marry up farther down the road. Marriage isn't about controlling the future, it's about making a plain statement about present intentions."

Spunky took this observation to heart. Present intentions are all we *ever* have. *Nothing* is under our control, in the end.

Which is why The Professor's call on the seventeenth of December didn't come as a shock. As soon as he told her that she and Elyon should pack up and come home immediately, she laughed. "Of course," she said.

"What do you mean, of course?" asked The Professor.

"Because we're making such progress and doing so well. Of course the plug's getting pulled."

"You're awfully young to have such a bitter outlook."

"My outlook is fine. It conforms to reality. Why are we shutting down? We're doing a good job here."

"Yes, you are. But the study depends on having at least three different locations that reach the threshold level of participation, and you're the only one I sent out that's reaching that threshold."

"You never told me what our threshold was."

"Two reasons, for that, Spunk. First, I didn't know that there *was* a threshold until my first benchmark with the foundation. Second, I wouldn't have told you anyway, because I find that when people know there's a threshold, they work hard until they get to that threshold and stop."

"I don't work that way."

"You're human, Spunk, so in fact you do, even when you think you don't. Come on back."

"What is it that you're not telling me?" asked Spunky.

"Come on back and I'll tell you in person that I'm not holding anything back."

"Will it be any truer then than it is now?" asked Spunky.

"Are you trying to burn all your bridges right now, Spunk?"

Spunky got downstairs only to find Elyon already

boxing up the equipment. "The Professor called you first?" she asked.

"I called him," said Elyon, "because eighty percent is a rational threshold for an excellent study."

"The goal was a hundred percent."

"And we're at ninety," said Elyon.

"Why did you rattle his cage?"

"I wanted to make sure we'd still be here at Christmas."

"How did that work out?" asked Spunky.

"He pulled the plug."

"Does this make any sense to you?" asked Spunky.

"None at all."

"Do you *like* this turn of events?"

"She'll stop loving me if I go away now," said Elyon. Spunky had never heard such misery in his voice.

"If she's smart, she'll keep loving you till you do something asinine like breaking up with her."

"Spunky, she's *not* smart," said Elyon.

"She's not *math* smart," said Spunky. "But she's way more human smart than you are. For instance, I bet *she* knows that the issue here isn't whether *she'll* still love *you*."

"Then what *is* the issue?"

"If you're still going to love *her,* then there *is* no issue."

"You mean she thinks *I'll* stop loving *her?*"

"That's right, Elyon. And do you know why she thinks that?"

"No. I keep my word. I've never broken my word to her."

"Because you're a man, Elyon. She knows you'll keep thinking of her as long as she lets you look down her blouse."

"I do not —"

Spunky didn't let him finish his outraged protest. "Elyon, if it isn't just temporary physical attraction due to daily proximity, if you really are committed to her, then she'll certainly wait until you send for her to come and marry you."

"Send for her where?" asked Elyon. "I don't have any income except this study, and if the study's over, I'm broke."

"Then you come back and the two of you live with her mother."

"I'm a scientist! I can't do any science without a grant."

"I know what you mean. Charles Darwin is still waiting for *his* grant, too."

"But his family was rich."

Spunky looked at him with barely controlled exasperation.

Elyon looked back at her for a long time. Until he realized. "Well, my family isn't *rich* rich."

"Slightly rich will do in this case. Do you think your family could tide you over during your first few months of marriage?"

"I wasn't going to tell them."

"Because you think they wouldn't like her?"

"I know that they'll *hate* her."

"I'm going to tell you why you're wrong," said Spunky.

"You don't *know* them. They're complete snobs, they hate everybody below the net worth of Bill Gates."

"Listen to me, Elyon. I don't have to know *your* parents. Because I know *human* parents, and your parents are of that species, aren't they?"

"On their good days," said Elyon sadly.

"Do you have any siblings?"

"My parents never sibbled me," said Elyon.

"So who is their only hope on God's green Earth to produce a grandchild for them, replicating their genes into the next generation?"

Elyon thought a moment. "Well, me, of course, but —"

"Do you think that at this moment, your parents actually believe that you will *ever* find a woman to make sweet love to you and raise your babies?"

Judging from Elyon's face, that hit him like a slap. But after a moment of stunned silence, he said, "Probably not."

"So when you announce to them that you'd like them to support you and your new bride until you can attach yourself to another grant, what will they say?"

"They'll ask, 'Where did she go to college?'" said Elyon.

"And what will you say back to them?" asked Spunky.

"Nowhere. She still has a couple of assignments to complete before they'll finally give her a high school diploma."

"Elyon, stop. Think. Do you understand that you're an idiot when it comes to human relations, and that the better you know people, the worse you get along with them?"

He thought for a moment. "Except Jozette. And Miz Eliza."

"OK, keep that knowledge right there." Spunky tapped his forehead. "Now listen to me. When your parents ask their snobby questions, like, Who are her parents? What does her father do? How much land do they own? Where did Jozette go to college? You will give the same answer to *all* those questions."

"There's no one thing that will answer *all* of them."

"You're wrong, Elyon, because you're an idiot. You will always be wrong, which is why you have to listen to me, right now. Your answer to all those questions will be, word for word, this: 'Dad. Mom.' Or Muzzy and Wuzzy, whatever you call them. 'Dad and Mom, Jozette has my baby in her and I want our child to have every chance at good health and a good education.'"

"She isn't pregnant," said Elyon. "We haven't ever done that."

"Elyon, I didn't tell you to tell your parents the *truth*. I told you how to answer them in order to get the results you want. But if lying bothers you, then make it true. There's at least one justice of the peace in Good Shepherd, North Carolina, and I know for a fact that there are fourteen separate ministers legally capable of marrying you to Jozette and her to you."

Elyon sat down. "They'd kill me."

"They won't kill you. They'll take three days to get over their shock and rage and disappointment, and then your father will start to say something about how to get the baby aborted or the marriage annulled, and your mother will put on her monster face and speak in her monster voice and here's what she'll say: 'That baby is my grandchild, and if you do anything to harm him or make it so he comes into this world as a bastard or an orphan you will spend the rest of your life looking for your balls, mister.'"

"My mother would never say that."

"I can promise you that she'll say that or she'll say worse. Because the minute you're married to Jozette and she passes a pregnancy test, that baby is the most important creature on this planet, as far as your parents are concerned. Especially your mother, because *she* is never going to have another shot at reproduction, and that's the biological imperative."

Elyon began to nod slowly, and then a very slight smile crept onto his lips. "You really are an expert at reading human nature, Spunky. I've seen you do it, time after time. And everybody who comes in here, they won't stop talking about how *wonderful* you are and how *smart* you are, and if I try to correct them they just get mad and stop talking to me."

"I'm glad to know that at least you *tried* to correct them about my being wonderful and/or smart."

"Truth matters to me, Spunk," he said. "If I didn't care about truth, I wouldn't be a scientist."

"What *would* you be? A NASCAR driver?"

"I don't have quick physical reflexes, Spunk. If I drove a race car, I would die."

"So here's my suggestion, Elyon. Instead of packing up this equipment, which is not needed *anywhere* until long after Christmas, you stay here, keep entering any samples that come in, and crunch even more numbers to see whatever it is that The Professor saw that made him pull the plug."

"He didn't see anything wrong with *our* data, it was the other populations that came up short."

"He's lying, Elyon."

"He can't—he doesn't—he's a *scientist.*"

"He's a money-spewing grant faucet, Elyon. He stopped being a scientist before he was out of graduate school."

"But he does science!"

"No, Elyon. He writes grants, he wins grants, and then he assigns the best graduate students and post-docs to do the science and write the papers, and he puts his name first on those papers so people like you think he's a scientist. So whatever reason he has for pulling the plug on us here in Good Shepherd, it has everything to do with his own reputation first, and keeping the grant-granters happy second, and covering up anything that will make him look bad third. Which means his reputation is first *and* third, and doing good science is down there just after keeping his wife happy enough not to divorce him and right before seeing his children so they can yell at him for being a lousy father."

"I thought you liked him."

"I do," said Spunky. "But he just pulled the plug on our study, and I don't want to leave Good Shepherd. Not now. Not just before Christmas."

"Are *you* pregnant with Eggie's baby?"

Spunky closed her eyes. "First, Elyon, I'm not. Second, Elyon, he doesn't lust after me the way you lust after Jozette, so I'm not really sure that he even *wants* to have a baby with me —"

"Oh, come on," said Elyon. "I've seen him kiss you. It's

like he's ready to explode. So gentlemanly, but his hands are, like, *quivering.*"

"It's cold."

"He's from around here, he's used to it. It's *you*. Why don't you come to the courthouse and get married the same time I marry Jozette?"

"Because first, Jozette will only marry you in a church. She's going to wear white and walk down the aisle and everybody's going to know she's marrying a brilliant scientist who loves her, and you know how they'll know that you love her? Because you're marrying her and she isn't even pregnant yet."

"A church."

"Do you believe in God?" Spunky asked.

"I'm a scientist. I don't even think about unfalsifiable hypotheses."

"Then you can't be worried that God will be irritated with you for stepping inside a church or for having the opinion that he probably doesn't exist."

"But what if Jozette wants me to be a Christian?"

"Anything against having your children baptized? Anything against having them raised as church-goers?"

"I was, and I turned out more or less sane."

"Less, but still. You get my point. Why would you need

to burden Jozette or anybody else by telling them your opinion that God is an unfalsifiable hypothesis?"

"So how would my going to a church to get married *not* be a lie?"

Spunky shook her head. "They don't make you promise that you believe in God, Elyon. Unless you're marrying a Catholic, and you're not. All that you promise is that you'll love, honor, and cherish her as long as you're both alive."

"How can I promise that? I can't guess the future."

Immediately Spunky remembered Miz Eliza's sermon on the topic. "Elyon, a promise is not a prediction. A promise means that it is, at this moment, your intention to stay married to and care for Jozette as long as you're alive. Will that be true, at the moment that you say it?"

Elyon nodded. "This is serious stuff."

"More serious than math," said Spunky.

"Nothing is more serious than math," said Elyon.

Spunky could not let that go unchallenged. "If human beings did not produce viable offspring and keep them alive until sexual maturity, who would there be on Earth to think about math?"

But Elyon was lost in his own brooding. "It really is going to make my parents mad. What if you're wrong and they cut me off without a penny?"

"Then you'll scramble and Jozette will scramble and between you you'll make enough to scrape by on until you get a job using that brilliant mind of yours and you come home with so much cash you can diaper your children with it."

So Elyon stayed behind and Spunky put an overnight bag into the van and headed out for the university. It was a long drive and she was already tired, so she stopped at a couple of oases—a Sheetz and a McDonald's—and walked around the building a couple of times to wake herself up. No caffeine—it didn't keep her awake, it just gave her a migraine—but the periodic walks were enough. She got to her apartment at the school, saw that her roommate had an overnight visitor, and spent the night on the couch. She didn't wish for a bed, she didn't wish for her pillow, she didn't wish for anything except to wake up and find Eggie somewhere nearby. Kitchen, yard, knocking at the door. Just ... nearby.

9

She didn't have an appointment with The Professor but she knew perfectly well that if he wanted to see you, he'd see you, and if he didn't, he'd tell you to make an appointment. No dates would ever work out until he *did* want to see you. Heretofore Spunky had accepted this is the way a "great man" worked; now it seemed to her to be monstrously narcissistic and borderline sociopathic.

Control yourself, Delilah, she told herself. He's the same man whose boots you would have licked upon demand six months ago. *He* hasn't changed, and he doesn't deserve to be despised just because *you* have.

The Professor saw her immediately. "I told you to come right back, but ... did you fly?"

"I drove back."

"'I' and not 'we'?"

"Elyon is closing up shop. I'll be back to help him load up the van."

"So this really is a flying visit. What's the urgency?"

"I did a lot of thinking on the drive up here, and I'm pretty sure you didn't lie to me at all. You didn't even conceal very much. We really are collecting way more data than the other places where you have teams gathering samples —"

"Had. They're already back."

"And you had our data, which you could rely on absolutely because, you know, Elyon."

"Obsessively thorough and accurate that boy is, and he chews up the numbers and spits out science."

"Ending this grant leaves him broke and jobless," said Spunky.

"That's why I sent unmarried post-docs on this one."

"Even single people need to eat and it's nice to have a warm place to sleep. But don't worry, he'll manage, and I agree, you don't keep a useless project going just to have full employment for grossly underpaid post-docs."

"I have to say I admired the work you did for all that gross underpayment," said The Professor.

"I admired it too," said Spunky. "Especially what Elyon kept finding in the GWAS."

"Oh? And what do you think he found?"

"Nothing," said Spunky.

"Well, exactly," said The Professor.

"Not what lay people mean by 'nothing,' of course," said Spunky. "Because he certainly did not come up with 'no reliable data.' Right?"

"Oh, of course not," said The Professor. "The data he delivered were definitely reliable." Did he look uncomfortable now? Spunky thought so. Maybe.

"What *I* saw was excellent data," said Spunky, "delving deeply into the whole population, and so the 'nothing' that Elyon came up with was a complete absence of associations between any statements on the DNA and the behavioral coming-and-going traits we were hoping to correlate."

"A distinction without a difference."

"You see, Professor, that's why I thought I detected a lie, because you have the reputation of being a scientist. Not a dilettante, not a hobbyist, and certainly not a grant-grinder. Yet a scientist does not, doesn't *ever*, regard reliable data that fails to show a correlation as 'nothing.' In fact, that's important evidence to show that the propensity to return to a particular home town is not a genetic trait, as was long thought to be true of migratory birds, but instead is culturally acquired."

"It isn't either-or," said The Professor.

"It's pretty close to either-or," said Spunky. "So it looks to me as if Elyon's first-rate number crunching gave us the perfectly publishable result that cultures can promote homebody behavior whether genes support it or not. Wouldn't you say that this is at least a preliminary indication?"

"Absence of evidence is not —"

"But evidence *isn't* absent. The evidence is present and it's clear. There is no statistically significant association between any of the examined portions of the DNA and the homing behavior."

"That is *not* a publication that I'm going to sign my name to," said The Professor.

"This morning when I got up I googled my way through the major donors to the foundation that gave you this grant, and it looks to me as if your donors would be unhappy if you published a paper saying that homing is a cultural trait in humans. Because that would mean that some cultures were better than others at bringing their members home again after allowing them to stray for a while."

"That's not even controversial."

"Because nobody's saying it. If *you* say it, backed up by our excellent fieldwork in Good Shepherd, North Carolina, it'll leave you without access to a bunch of very deep pockets that you've been dipping your hand in."

"You're coming perilously close to —"

"Lese majestie? Only if you're a king. Treason? Only if you're a country. Blasphemy? I'm pretty sure you aren't God."

"After all our years of association, Spunk, I'm sorry that you can think of me like this."

"Professor," said Spunky, "Elyon and I are going to finish collecting *our* data in *our* population-wide study of Good Shepherd North Carolina. Then we're going to publish *our* data in a paper from which you may remove your name but to which you may not add it in any position except last."

"That's not happening, young —"

"Oh, spare me the fake parental wrath. That paper can either say nothing at all about this little glitch in our funding, or it can say that because the data was not what you desired, you pulled the plug. That amounts to hiding unfavorable data, and that's a serious sin in our line of work."

"My line of work," said The Professor. "You don't *have* a line of work, after this conversation."

"You can probably block the paper's publication in any of the peer-reviewed journals, but it won't change the fact that all those reviewing peers will read the truth about you and the way you deliberately skew data to meet the expectations of your donors. As a last resort, we'll put it online and call a press conference. But wouldn't it be better if we published it as science instead of as gossip? Wouldn't it be better if the paper had your name on it because the grant was *not* interrupted, and because you're the kind of scientist who publishes the data with a thorough analysis, no matter whether somebody's balloon gets punctured by it?"

The Professor sat there gazing off into space. What a shame he gave up the pipe a few years ago, or he'd look like he was posing for a J.R.R. Tolkien lookalike contest.

"I'm sorry that this conversation had to be adversarial," he finally said. "But that was my fault, not yours, because I was acting to cut off all conversation instead of listening to you. Your points are well taken. It's not about appearances—not *just* about appearances. But my zeal to maintain my reputation for doing studies that are worth funding got in the way of my thinking and acting like a scientist. You reminded me of my duty, and I will now act accordingly."

Spunky tried to decide whether this capitulation was real or if she was being conned.

"As of this moment, the funding for your GWAS is reinstated. How close are you to finishing?"

"As Elyon told you, we're at about ninety percent. I think

it's worth a few more weeks to get as close to a hundred as we can."

"Then you may have those weeks."

"Then I'll head back and tell Elyon to unpack." Spunky rose to her feet.

"That really is what you came back for?"

"Also, I wanted to see what small town life looks like— because I've learned that academia is one of the smallest small towns anywhere."

"Fair point," said The Professor.

"And the genome GWAS is going to show a lot of things that aren't relevant to the study, that I would like to see through to their conclusion."

"It's unethical to share the raw data with —"

"Don't worry, I know the rules at least as well as you do."

All the way back to the van, she half expected to have some goons from campus security stop her and put her in a dentist's chair and hold a drill to her teeth and repeat, over and over, Is it safe?

She didn't even go back to her apartment to pick up her bag. She wanted to return to Good Shepherd before dark.

10

This time, when she got sleepy, it was broad daylight. She pulled into a gas station, filled up the van to the tune of more than fifty bucks, and then slept for half an hour. She woke up when her ringtone insisted.

Elyon said, "Well?"

"Well what?"

"Did you find out what's going on!"

"I'm halfway back now. I was going to tell you as soon as —"

"Do you see that thing my voice is coming out of right now?" he shouted through the phone. "It works in both directions."

"I should have ... I should have called you. I don't know what I was thinking. I'm really tired."

"We're talking now," said Elyon. "So you can tell me now."

"The grant is reinstated. I mean, our part of it. We're going to finish up in Good Shepherd."

At first Spunky couldn't understand why Elyon didn't say anything. Then she heard just enough breathing and smacking noise to know that Jozette was there, heard the good news, and there was some serious happy-kissing going on. She ended the call.

Well, that's fine. I did my job. And now you can be happy with the best good fortune that ever came to you in your generally obnoxious life, Elyon.

She immediately regretted the thought. A lot of Elyon's obnoxiousness came from his upbringing, the world of snobbery and condescension of his parents. And a lot of it came from his genuine fascination with math and science, which made him oblivious to a lot of human things going on around him. But since he started eating with Jozette, he had been noticing more than he used to. He was becoming human. So not only would *he* be happier with Jozette, everyone else would be happier with *him*.

The catnap had done its job, even if Elyon's phone call *did* cut it short. She was back on the road in no time, tank full, determined to get up into Good Shepherd while there was still light in the sky.

If I were in a crappy movie, this is when I'd crash the car, thought Spunky, as she woke up for the second time. Each time it had been only a micro-sleep, a tiny nod. She hadn't left her lane. She wasn't tailgating anybody and there weren't a bunch of cars behind her wishing she'd speed up. She was alone on this road.

This unfamiliar road, with sudden turns. With my brain cutting out every five minutes no matter how much I flex my muscles on the steering wheel or sing fake lyrics to songs I don't know or yell back at talk radio. Bouncing up and down on the seat doesn't keep me awake. Thinking about getting back to Eggie doesn't fill me with adrenaline. If anything it makes me feel more complacent and relaxed.

There was a light shining in her eyes. It was night.

The car wasn't moving. She must have fallen asleep and crashed. The person shining the light had to be a cop or an EMT.

"Are you OK, Spunky?"

It wasn't a cop. It was Eggie. Elyon must have called him when she wasn't home with the van by dark.

"Did I crash?" she asked.

"Very, very gently, in a parking place on a scenic overlook," he said.

It took her a moment to realize what he had said.

124

"So I parked, then."

"I'm glad you left the window open."

"I was letting in cold air to keep me awake," she said.

"Didn't work, but it did mean you heard me when I talked to you. Better than breaking the van window."

She closed her eyes again.

"Here's the deal," said Eggie. "I'm helping you out of that van, and you're going to take about five steps, leaning on me, to my car. Then I'm going to drive you home because I am actually awake."

"OK," she answered, wondering what he had said.

"I hope your quick trip back to the university was worth it," he said.

"Was," she murmured as they took those steps to his car.

"Because I thought you were really gone. Van missing, you missing, not even a note."

"Sorry," she said. "So mad."

"I wasn't mad," he said. "But I felt like I had lost the most precious thing in my life. I thought you were gone."

"I'm back," she said. "Didn't Elyon tell you? We still have our grant. Stay through Christmas at least."

"Good thing," said Eggie. "Wouldn't want to miss the dueling pageants."

He closed her door, making sure she didn't have anything

dangling out of the car. Then he walked around and got in. His door closing woke her up again. "Was I asleep?" she asked.

"No more interrogation," he said. "You can sleep now."

"Thanks," she said.

A few moments later, as if in a dream, she heard him say, "I want to marry you, Spunky. I know what that means. But I can leave Good Shepherd. I can go wherever you need to go. I'm with you for the long haul. Even when you're asleep, I'll be awake. Is that OK with you?"

And in the dream, if it was a dream, she said, "What if I want to stay in Good Shepherd and wife it up with you?"

Then she really was asleep.

He carried her up the stairs to her apartment and didn't bump her head on any walls and corners and banisters. She was impressed, because by now she had slept enough to be completely awake. But she kept her eyes closed, mostly, because it felt good to be carried.

"I'm not going to undress you for bed," said Eggie as he laid her on top of her covers. "Not my job, and you're not drunk anyway."

"Am so," she said.

"Not even a little," he said.

"Drunk on being carried upstairs by the man I love," she said.

"Now, that's just maudlin," he said. "Fortunately, you won't remember saying it in the morning."

"Will too," she said.

"Tomorrow I'm going to pry into whatever dream you were having in the car, because all of a sudden, out of nowhere, you spoke up, clear as day, and you said—no, it was just a dream, not fair of me to —"

"Did I say, 'What if I want to stay in Good Shepherd and wife it up with you'?"

He didn't answer.

"It made sense in my dream because *you* said you could leave Good Shepherd and go wherever I need to go. But I don't like science anymore. There's too much meanness and fakery and lying and backstabbing."

"You can't give up your career."

"A career is what you look back on. What you live is a life."

"Wisdom from a sleeping woman."

"Best kind," she said.

"Just for your information, what you thought I said in the car? That wasn't a dream. I just thought you couldn't hear me."

"So the part where you said you wanted to marry me?"

"I've been saying that for weeks, every way I know how except words."

"I liked hearing the words. But it takes a real coward to propose to a woman in her sleep."

"Women like you don't marry men like me," said Eggie.

"And that's what's wrong with this lousy world," said Spunky. "Go away, I've got sleep to do."

11

On the twentieth of December, Eggie drove her out to the crop-duster airport and took her into a locked hangar and put her in the co-pilot's seat.

"I can't fly this, Eggie," she said.

"Then it's a good thing I can."

It was a propeller plane, and he flew it to Atlanta, and they went to a jewelry store with a huge display of engagement and wedding bands, and he said, "Pick one."

He suggested a couple with good-sized but not flamboyant diamonds, one with a huge emerald "because Scarlett O'Hara had one," and he seemed a little disappointed when she chose a simple band with no stone at all.

"That's a wedding band," he said.

"Don't need an engagement ring," she said.

"How will everybody know you're mine?" he asked.

"Everybody who matters already knows," she said. "Besides, you'll be attached to my hand most of the time."

"So just the simple band," he said. "Do I have to tell you just how big a killing I made on Wall Street?"

"How many potholes could you fix for the price of a diamond?" she asked.

He laughed. "You're even crazier than I am," he said.

The ring didn't even have to be resized. The jeweler seemed disappointed.

"This won't be our last visit here," Eggie said to him. "But the lady wants the kind of ring that will never make any of our friends jealous."

"The plain band will mean that I'm married to you," said Spunky. "Let 'em eat their hearts out."

12

It was Christmas Eve, a couple of hours before the dueling pageants. Everything was ready, the town was packed with day tourists and all the rentable rooms in town had been rented.

Elyon called Spunky into his clinic and tried to keep Eggie from coming with them.

"Sorry," said Eggie. "We're attached at the hand."

"Well, I didn't bring Jozette and she's my *wife*, so this isn't even fair."

"Quickest church wedding ever arranged for a bride who wasn't pregnant," said Eggie.

"Enthusiasm," said Elyon.

"So what's this discovery?" asked Spunky.

"You have to promise not to tell anyone," said Elyon to

Eggie. "I wouldn't even *ask* Jozette not to tell her mother, and there's no way Miz Eliza could keep it to herself, so I'm not telling my own wife. OK?"

"I won't tell him and he won't tell me," said Spunky. "Before and after we're married."

"I know what the division in the town was all about," said Elyon.

Elyon's hand was now holding a couple of printouts, with handwritten names above the data identification numbers.

"You did something unethical with our data," said Spunky.

"Yes I did," said Elyon, "which is why it cannot be known. Also because if anyone heard what it says, I might be lynched."

"No you wouldn't," said Eggie, "but please stop the preambling and just tell us."

Elyon handed the papers to Spunky. They were comparisons of several people's DNA.

"He's not related to any of the relatives on his father's side," said Spunky. "His closest living relative, since he never had children, is the Baby Jesus. The other Baby Jesus."

"Born on the same day. Half-brothers," said Spunky.

Eggie buried his face in his hands. "Sibling rivalry from the start," he said.

"A betrayed woman who couldn't stand the thought of

her husband's bastard playing the Baby Jesus in place of her own legitimate child," said Spunky.

"A lot of people prayed for that sick baby to live," said Eggie, "but I wonder if anybody was praying for him to die."

"No," said Spunky. "She was a Christian woman, and she hadn't committed any sin at all. Except wanting her own little boy to be the Baby Jesus in the 1930 pageant."

"You're right. She didn't wish death on a helpless baby," said Eggie.

"Maybe just a slightly longer illness so the doctors would veto his participation," said Spunky with a smile.

"Kind of a therapeutic illness," said Elyon.

"It was very sensitive of you," Spunky said to Elyon, "to keep this a secret."

"I just think, 'What would Spunky do?' and then I actually do it."

"Keep that up," said Eggie. "I do it, too."

"You do not," said Spunky. "You should have heard me reaming out the Professor. I was not Christian. I was not kind."

"It brought you back to Good Shepherd," said Eggie. "So clearly you were on God's errand."

Halfway through the pageants, Spunky made Eggie walk her around to watch the other one.

"Are they using the same script?"

"Hasn't been changed in more than a hundred years," said Eggie.

"Right to the second, their timing is identical."

"Didn't used to be," said Eggie. "When I was little, each pageant tried to drown the other one out and throw off their timing. But now they almost seem to be putting them on in stereo."

"In harmony," said Spunky.

"When does Santa Claus come in?" asked Elyon.

Merry Christmas

JAN - - 2019